THE VIOLETS OF
USAMBARA

Mary Soderstrom

THE VIOLETS OF
USAMBARA

Cormorant Books

Canada Council   Conseil des Arts
for the Arts   du Canada

The publisher gratefully acknowledges the support of the
Canada Council for the Arts and the Ontario Arts Council
for its publishing program. We acknowledge the financial support
of the Government of Canada through the Book Publishing
Industry Development Program (BPIDP) for our publishing activities.

Printed and bound in Canada

LIBRARY AND ARCHIVES CANADA CATALOGUING IN PUBLICATION

Soderstrom, Mary, 1942–
The violets of Usambara /Mary Soderstrom

ISBN 978-1-897151-25-9

I. Title.

PS8587.O415V56 2008   C813'.54   C2007-906470-1

Cover design: Angel Guerra/Archetype
Text design: Tannice Goddard/
Soul Oasis Networking
Cover image: Angel Guerra/Archetype
Author Photo: Ron Diamond
Printer: Friesens

The story "Violettes d'Usambara" was published in the January/February 2000
issue of The North American Review (Vol. 285, No. 1). Parts of it are found in this novel.

CORMORANT BOOKS INC.
215 SPADINA AVENUE, STUDIO 230, TORONTO, ON CANADA M5T 2C7
www.cormorantbooks.com

*For the good people at the Amani Nature Reserve in the
East Usambara Mountains of Tanzania*

They both agreed that in an ideal world, Louise would have gone to
Burundi, not Thomas. Africa was her continent. For years she'd kept
tabs on it, raised money for it, grown its flowers. But Louise did not
travel well, and it was Thomas who was needed. Or so Louise said.

The trip from Bujumbura to the camp took about four hours, and
Thomas held on to the panic bar in the Jeep the whole way. He did not
realize how tightly he was gripping it until the Jeep finished threading
its way through the lanes that ran between the shelters and came to a
stop where the roadway ended. He expected his knees to be stiff, to
creak a bit as he stepped out of the vehicle — that had been happening
lately, a sign of aging that he didn't like to think about — but the
frozen muscles in his hand were something new. In the end, he had to
take his other hand and pry his fingers loose. He said nothing about
this. The other observers couldn't be more than forty, while the drivers
of the two Jeeps and the four young men riding shotgun with AK-47s
looked barely out of their teens — AK-47s are the boy soldier's weapon,
and Thomas wondered briefly, and not for the first time, if they were

any worse than the guns Oerlikon made. None of the others seemed to mind the drive up the relatively well-paved road north of Bujumbura and along the muddy track that led to the refugee camp.

The drivers parked the Jeeps just inside the barbed-wire fence that enclosed the camp's headquarters. The camp itself, Thomas knew, was no longer supposed to be very dangerous. It was full of people who, in recent months, had poured across the border from Zaire to the west. The other four camps they were scheduled to visit were farther away, up in the hills, and sheltered people who were not refugees as such, but exiles in their own country. Bailey, the man from Witness International, said the outside world had heard little news from any of the camps in the last seven months because of the embargo. Whatever information Thomas and his group reported would be very important because current conditions in those camps were completely unknown. "But this camp is run by the UN High Commission for Refugees, supported by three non-government organizations," he said. "Consider this a practice run."

Practice run, Thomas thought, as he stood next to the Jeep, stretching his arms and working his fingers. The others in his group also stayed close to the vehicles as they took stock of the camp, which housed, Bailey said, about 10,000 people.

Most of the shelters reminded Thomas of the longhouses North American Indians used to build, with silhouettes like a loaf of bread. These structures appeared to be constructed of branches woven together to form an arching roof high enough for a person to stand up in the middle. They had no windows and no chimneys, and, since it was the rainy season, all were covered with bright blue, orange or dirty white plastic tarps. Inside, they would be dark and airless and hot.

The tarps must have come from the NGOs and the UNHCR, Thomas guessed. Same thing for a few small tents he saw here and there, and for the big tent inside the compound. Where did the material to make the shelters come from? The land was bare of vegetation — Thomas could see no trees, no bushes, only shelters scattered in a haphazard pattern that went on and on, seemingly without end. It wasn't until his eyes lifted toward the hills on the other side of the river that he saw, kilometres away in Zaire, mountains that looked green and, perhaps, tree-covered. Here, there was only mud. Mud and people and smoke rising from their cooking, he thought. But then, he realized, not long ago there would have been jungle here too, or forest or brush. Everything must have been cut down to make shelters or to burn for cooking fires. The landscape had been transformed as much as these people's lives had been by the conflict between Hutus and Tutsis.

The temptation to think about lives transformed flooded over him, but, as he had reminded himself before, he was not here because of what might have happened in his past. That was nothing — nothing at all — compared to the tragedies that had played out here.

He squinted against the sun. The equator ran a couple of hundred kilometres to the north, through Kenya, Rwanda, Zaire. The seasons changed here — rainy and not rainy — but the times of sunrise and sunset varied no more than thirty-five minutes over the year. At home in Montreal, with the equinox approaching, the sun at noon would only be halfway up the sky, but here, the midday sunlight fell straight down. It circumvented his sunglasses — he needed a hat. He should have bought one of those floatable cotton ones made in Canada, but he hadn't thought to. Nor had Louise.

Louise. The competence of Louise — his Loulou. Another train of thought that would lead nowhere. Better to try to get the measure of this place.

His ears were still filled with the sound of the Jeep, of the wind rushing past them. Around him, he was aware of the noises of the camp, the chatter of children, a woman shouting, two hammers pounding out of sync with each other, more wind, but also the absence of other sounds — no machines, no vehicles, no generators. Even the smells that hit him were ancient — woodsmoke, rotting vegetation, a hint of sewage.

From behind him, Thomas heard movement, and he turned to see a slight white woman with short white hair come out of the

13

headquarters tent. She was smiling as she looked past him toward Bailey, who was taking things out of the back of the Jeep and handing them to the driver.

"Well, look who's here," she said coming forward, her arms outstretched. "What took you so long?" She only came up to Bailey's shoulder, her two hands gripping his elbows as she beamed up at him. She was wearing hiking boots and khaki pants like many other people working for NGOs, but the way her white short-sleeved shirt was buttoned all the way to the collar set her apart from the other female aid workers Thomas had met so far.

Bailey looked surprised at the warmth of her welcome. "Well, we got here," he said. He turned slightly, out of her grasp, and began to introduce the others — the tall, lanky fellow from the Mennonite Missionary Service, the dark-haired woman from the Witness International office in New York, and Thomas Brossard from Canadian Catholic Overseas Charities.

The small woman smiled at the other two, but when Bailey came to Thomas, her expression shifted. "Thomas Brossard," she said, pronouncing it the French way. "The Honourable Thomas Brossard," she added in English. "Louise's husband. I heard she'd been campaigning to get you involved."

She was one of Louise's religious friends, a nun, Thomas immediately realized. He might have been the one with the political career, but Louise's shadow extended all the way here.

"So you came to see what we're doing?" the nun asked once hands were shaken and smiles exchanged. Her question appeared to be general, but she looked straight at Thomas. "We'll show you. You'll have a lot to report. I promise."

Before, in his other life, he had represented his government on many trade missions and at dozens of conferences. Inspection visits like this would begin with a greeting, followed by a walk-about and a chance to talk to a worker, a school child or a small-businessman.

The real information would come out later. Thomas thought he had learned how to look around edges for the truth, how to tease news about the real situation from a web of official words. He was prepared to do much the same on this trip, even though he was here as a private citizen.

At lunch in the headquarters tent — bottled water and vegetable stew — the nun explained that this was the second wave of refugees to use the camp. It first sheltered Hutus fleeing Rwanda in fear of retribution of the genocide there, but Burundi's Tutsi government had pushed them back home. Now the camp was full of Tutsis from Zaire who wanted to get away from the growing trouble there.

The armed guards who had come with them from Bujumbura walked in front as the nun led Thomas and the other observers down the camp's winding paths. The water tanks and electric lines had been put up during the first period, she said, and luckily no one had removed that infrastructure while the camp was empty. It had been a relatively simple matter to bring back generators and fill the tanks with water when the refugees from Zaire arrived.

"The shelters were still standing for the most part, too," she went on, stopping by the entrance of one where women were sitting, resting from the midday heat. "People had taken what they could with them, but the basic huts were still here. And since we've got fewer refugees than there were then, crowding is not as bad."

The women looked up at the little group of whites, blinking at the light. One of them said something and the others giggled.

The nun ignored them. She pointed to a small boy leaning against his mother, who stared up at Thomas. "He's thin," she said, "but notice that he doesn't have a pot-belly or scabby skin. He's not seriously malnourished." The boy scratched the back of his left calf with his right foot. "And see how tall he is. He's probably three if he's still hanging around the women and not running with the other kids, but he's as tall as a kindergartner."

The man from the Mennonite services nodded. "They're being well treated, is that what you're telling us?" he asked. He had pulled a small notebook out of his shirt pocket and was taking notes.

Thomas looked around for other children to compare with the boy. He saw women with babies in slings on their backs and a couple of bare-legged seven- or eight-year-old girls in short, tattered dresses. But before he could spy any boys, he was hit by a choking smell. Sewage, the revolting smell of human waste, left to fester in a dark place.

The nun coughed too. "They are cleaning out the latrine pits," she said. "We've had some trouble with them. Usually it's not this bad."

"Sanitation is always a problem," the Mennonite man said, covering his face with a bandana. "You haven't had any cholera?"

"No," the nun answered, and began an explanation of the sanitary arrangements as she walked quickly down the lane, away from the smell.

Thomas didn't follow immediately. He was hunched over, fighting back nausea. He fumbled a Kleenex from his back pocket as he gagged, his mouth filling with bile. He spat, and scrubbed at his mouth with the tissue, trying to clear the taste away. For several seconds he squatted there, willing his heart to stop pounding and the sweat pouring down his face to subside.

By the time the smell had dissipated a bit and he felt he could go on, the others were almost out of sight. He knew he should hurry to catch up, but a flash of red, bright against the browns and tans of the earth, caught his eye. Boys were running and shouting down a path that branched off from the one Thomas's group was on. Thomas heard a cheer go up and saw another red T-shirt flash by.

Kids having a good time? A soccer game in this heat? Strange in this strange place. No one else seemed to be moving — the women were resting, a couple of old men sat in the shade, heat bounced off the plastic tarps.

The boys disappeared from his line of sight, and before he knew it, Thomas found himself on their trail, wondering at the contrast between their apparent joy and the lethargy of the rest of the camp. He threaded his way between the huts, carefully stepping around the puddles taking up much of the path, thankful that the smell of stale ashes and mould had replaced the stench of sewage.

As he came closer to the end of the path, an expanse of mud appeared beyond the group of shelters. In the middle, Thomas saw eight or ten gangly, pre-adolescent boys dressed in coloured T-shirts chasing a much smaller boy. Thomas tried to catch sight of the ball the smaller one must be dribbling amid the pumping legs. Strange, Thomas thought, he's not trying to pass or shoot at whatever they're using for goalposts. Indeed, it was only when two boys pounced that Thomas realized what was happening. The smaller boy fell and the others stopped. They shouted as the two front-runners began kicking the smaller boy.

There was no ball. It was no game.

Despite the heat, despite the residual smells, Thomas rushed out onto the expanse of mud, startling the boys who turned and fled. The injured boy lay on the ground, his knees pulled up and his back curved forward, his forearms covering his gut. He was not crying. Thomas heard Bailey yelling, "Brossard, what the hell do you think you're doing?"

"You don't understand," the nun said when Thomas, Bailey, the boy and the armed man had rejoined the group. "Here you must not go off by yourself. A well-travelled man like you should know better."

"But the boy ..." Thomas began. The child had blood streaming down his face and held his right arm in front of him at an angle that Thomas was sure was unnatural. He was walking, however, supported on his left side by the guard.

"The boy will be looked after. We can handle cuts and bruises," the nun said. Her voice was curt, authoritative, like that of Sister Benedict, his third-grade teacher in Boston. "Now, do you want to see the rest of the camp or not?"

He followed along after that. No one mentioned what had happened again, not during the meal they shared with the medical staff in the evening, nor the couple of hours they spent sitting inside the compound, listening to a lay missionary play the guitar and sing.

The next morning, they toured the fields outside the camp proper, where people had begun to plant beans. The nun talked about food aid, what could be produced here and the number of malnourished babies who had received supplementary feeding, while the others took notes. Thomas — who'd left his notebook back at the hotel — nodded, telling himself he would remember all this, that he would write it all down when they arrived back in Bujumbura. What he really wanted to know was the boy's story.

On the way back from the fields, Thomas made a point of walking beside the nun so he could ask about him. "Do you have any idea why the bigger boys attacked him?" he asked as they passed the tiny plots.

She didn't look at him, nor did she answer his question. "The boy will be all right," she said evenly, calmly, as if there were much more in this world to worry about than conflicts among boys. "His aunt is looking after him. He's a lucky one, actually. He's lost his parents, but he has several relatives in the camp." Then she turned to say something else to Bailey.

"No, wait," Thomas said. He fished in his pocket for the hidden compartment where he carried extra US money. "Here," he said, pulling out a bill. "Give this to him."

She took the bill and looked at it — twenty US dollars, Thomas saw; he hadn't looked before.

"Give it to him," Thomas repeated.

"I'll see that it is used properly," she said.

For just a second, Thomas wondered if he should press her, make sure that the money wouldn't disappear into the general welfare fund, but Bailey quickly took him by the arm and reminded him that they had to get going if they were to get back to Bujumbura before curfew.

Half-grown boys and refugees; Thomas thought about them as he held tightly to the panic bar of the Jeep that sped back to the city. Memory is much faster, however. All our memories are hiding inside our brains, ready to be tapped at the speed of light if the right signal is given. In a nanosecond the thought of half-grown boys and refugees sent Thomas back to Montreal in 1994, six months after he lost the election. He was still looking for work then, and was not pleased when his newly retired mother announced that she was coming from Boston to visit.

"I didn't want to leave town for the first little while," she said on the phone. "Nobody knows how things work the way a school secretary does. But now the new one is broken in, so I will come to see you."

Thomas was not pleased, but he had trouble telling Louise why. It boiled down to the fact that he did not want to hear his mother sigh over the way his career had crumbled. He did not want to hear her say that it had been a mistake for his father to send him to board at Collège Brébeuf the year of their divorce. He did not want to hear her complain that he would have done better if he had stayed in the US. He did not want her to speculate aloud on what he might have become if he'd stayed in a first-rate country instead of allowing himself to be ensnared by a second-rate one.

In the past, she had never listened when he'd protested that, by many people's standards, he'd done very well. The last time they talked, he added that he was tired of hearing Americans claim the moral high road as their own. That was shortly after Bill Clinton was elected and he and Hillary were trying to set up universal Medicare in the States, but the plan was going nowhere. "For Christ's sake," Thomas said, "we've had it here for thirty years. Just what the heck are you doing down there? People are dying because they haven't got insurance."

She could not answer that, but now with Thomas's own electoral defeat behind him and the future unclear, he didn't want to have to defend himself.

Louise insisted they be hospitable to her anyway. "She's an old woman," she said. "Just because she's wrong is no reason for us to be mean." He suspected she was right, as she so often was, so he agreed that they take his mother out to dinner and that they tell the kids be polite.

To complicate things, the evening before Mrs. Brossard arrived, their younger son, Sylvain, asked if he could invite his friend Benjamin over for the weekend.

Thomas was in the other room, ready to call out a summary "no." But Louise didn't answer immediately, and the weight of her silence made him hesitate. Finally, she asked, "He's the one whose father was killed last week?"

"Yes," Thomas heard Sylvain say, and listened to more silence. Of course, Thomas thought, *Le Devoir* had a story about the family on Wednesday when the news of the bloodbath in Rwanda began to come out. Benjamin's father was a Tutsi from a *colline* north of Kigali, who'd met Benjamin's mother — a woman from a small town in farming country, south of Montreal — when he'd been training as an agronomist at Université Laval in Quebec City. He had gone back to Rwanda in January, and his wife and their four children had been scheduled to move there as soon as the school year ended.

When Sylvain finally spoke, his voice broke the way it had the year before, when it began to change. "His mother wants to take the little kids down to their grandparents' in the country," he said. "But Benjamin's got tests next week, he won't be able to study down there." There was a pause. "And besides, Maman, he's so sad ..."

"In that case, of course Benjamin can stay with us," Thomas heard Louise say, all hesitation pushed aside. Later, Louise asked that Thomas prepare his mother — she would not allow there to be a scene in front of the boy.

Officially, Mrs. Brossard was in favour of equality for everybody. "We're all God's children," she'd told Thomas when he was a boy. After his parents' divorce, she had chosen to remain in a neighbourhood that teetered on the brink of complete racial change. She had worked long and dedicated years in a parochial school that had originally taught the children of Irish- and Franco-Americans, and then found a second life as the school of choice for the children of hard-working African-American families. She wasn't unsophisticated, she wasn't mean. She considered herself tolerant.

More than once, though, she had said she really didn't think that the coloured wanted to mix with the whites anymore than the other way around. Never to Thomas's knowledge had she sat down for a meal with a person of colour in a social setting. The cafeteria at her school and the restaurants where she sometimes treated herself had been integrated for decades but she had never been a guest at a table where a person of colour was welcomed as an equal or friend. | 11

Thomas told his mother about Benjamin over breakfast on Saturday morning before the boy arrived. She listened politely to his explanation of the friendship between the two boys and the tragedy that had befallen Benjamin's father. She didn't respond right away, but seemed to consider various reactions as Thomas watched with apprehension. "Well of course, I'll be glad to meet any friend of Sylvain's," she said finally. She shook her shoulders in a tiny shiver. "The poor thing."

Thomas smiled when he heard that. Perhaps it would be all right. Benjamin was a handsome boy and, possibly just as important where Mrs. Brossard was concerned, not very dark. When he arrived at the house in the middle of the afternoon, Thomas made a point of introducing him to Mrs. Brossard before he and Sylvain disappeared to listen to music in Sylvain's room. Benjamin politely shook Mrs. Brossard's hand, told her he was *enchanté*, and Thomas saw her smile at him.

They neglected, however, to prepare her for their eldest son's girlfriend — Anh-Louise was standing next to Richard outside the restaurant when they drove up. When Richard introduced her to his grandmother, Thomas saw a quick look of panic pass over the old woman's face as she took in the tiny girl — her slanted eyes, her sleek black hair, her pale skin — before she regained her calm and accepted the girl's handshake and greeting kisses with a careful smile.

The dinner itself was deceptively pleasant. Sylvain and Benjamin talked mostly to Richard and Anh-Louise about subjects that Thomas didn't catch, while their daughter, Marielle, told her grandmother stories about medical school. Thomas watched the pleasure with which Louise ate, he noticed that Sylvain was trying to make Benjamin laugh, he saw Richard take Anh-Louise's hand and hold it on top of the table where everyone could see. Then he heard his mother talking to him.

"The girl, where is she from?" she asked in English, the language she had always used with him for official business when he was growing up.

"Anh-Louise you mean?" he answered, stalling a little, wondering just what his mother was getting at. "She was born here. Louise met her mother in a prenatal class, as a matter of fact. But if you're asking about her ancestry, it's Vietnamese."

His mother nodded. "I should have known," she said. "She is very pretty. Richard seems to be very fond of her." She paused for a second. "Her family, are they some of those boat people?"

"Boat people?" Thomas asked, although he suspected where her thinking was headed.

"You know, those refugees from Vietnam that came flooding in," she said, giving her shoulders a little shake, as if willing unpleasantness away. "So poor, so many of them ..."

Thomas forced himself to laugh, cutting her off. "I don't think so," he said. "They seem to be quite well off."

"And the boy. You said his father was killed in some trouble in Africa?"

"Yes," he said. "An inter-ethnic clash."

His mother once again shook her shoulders, this time as if a great cold wave of disgust had flowed over her. "Savages. All of them, all over the world," she said. "Just goes to show you how difficult it is to civilize people."

Thomas looked around quickly to see if anyone else had heard.

Only one had.

Benjamin's eyes met Thomas's across the table.

Thomas's memories fled as the Jeeps paused before turning into the hotel compound. Five or six boys stood outside the closed grillwork gate. The young man riding shotgun jumped out of their Jeep, shouting at the gatekeeper, who seemed reluctant to open up. Then he moved to unsling his weapon. The boys did not notice, they were looking inside the Jeep, pushing their faces next to the window, pointing to their mouths, crying, "*Faim, faim*, hungry, hungry."

Thomas gripped the panic bar tightly. They were tall, skinny boys, about the same age as the one in the camp, only a few years younger than Benjamin and Sylvain had been.

A uniformed guard with his own AK–47 strode across the hotel's courtyard, gesturing with his weapon for the boys to move aside. Their guard turned to point his weapon at the boys, who took a few steps back. The gatekeeper opened the gate. The Jeep could enter, and Bailey grunted in satisfaction that they had returned safely.

The boys' eyes stayed with Thomas when he settled down for the night in his comfortable hotel room, his luxurious room, complete with king-size bed, shiny porcelain toilet and bidet. There were no unsanitary latrines here, no bad smells, he thought as he drifted off to sleep in the protective darkness. He was safe, he must not let the eyes intrude upon his sleep.

In the morning, the eyes still troubled him, but he knew he must banish them to focus on the work at hand. Even though it was Sunday, the group of observers were supposed to set off in late morning for a camp for internally displaced persons, or IDPs. When Thomas came down for breakfast a little before nine, however, Théophile, the hotel manager, had a message from Bailey.

"There has been a small problem concerning transport that Mr. Bailey has gone to rectify. He said to tell you and the others that you have the morning off," he said, as he led Thomas through the covered area that served as a bar in the afternoon and evenings. At the edge of the pool, six tables had been set with cutlery and white tablecloths under an awning.

"You are the first to arrive," Théophile said, pulling out a chair for Thomas at an otherwise empty table. "Would you like coffee? We also have croissants this morning, which is a treat for us these days."

Bailey had said to expect only the basics, even in the hotel, because of the embargo. For six months, the surrounding African countries had not allowed shipments into Burundi in an attempt to force the government and rebel forces to the bargaining table.

"Bujumbura used to be famous for its bakers, its butter and its fish," Théophile continued, standing erect, immaculate in his jacket, tie and crisp light blue shirt, even though the heat was already rising. "But last week we couldn't find sugar at the market and the fishermen haven't been allowed on the lake for weeks." He leaned forward, confidentially, smiling. "However, this Sunday, we have *confiture Bonne Maman* to go with the croissants. Imported from France. The chef's special stock."

Thomas nodded at the man's proud smile. "Very good," he said. "And tea, please. With milk and sugar, if you have it." Then he looked around at the other tables.

Families sat at two of them already, and as Thomas watched, the other three tables quickly filled with well-dressed people, looking as if they had been to early Mass and were now free to enjoy Sunday brunch. The women, without exception, were lovely — slender, tall, with rich brown skin, wearing dresses of brightly coloured fabric, or wrapped in long skirts worn with jacket-like blouses. The men were also tall, but two of them had round bellies that even their well-cut jackets couldn't camouflage. Thomas counted twelve children from babyhood to near-adolescence. The boys wore white shirts and ties,

14

and the girls, bright dresses with fluffy skirts. His own children had never been better dressed, and Thomas's memories of Sundays when they were young rang with their noise — back chat, teasing, minor conflicts that always exasperated Louise. These children appeared much more serious than his had ever been as they ate their croissants and drank their chocolate.

He told himself he should remember this; he should begin writing in the journal Louise had put in his suitcase. She would appreciate a little description of the Sunday morning crowd. He should check out the cathedral too.

His thoughts were interrupted by the sudden awareness that someone was standing just to his left. He turned to see a boy of about nine carrying a kind of instrument — a curved piece of wood with strings. No one else appeared to notice him, even when he began to sing a mournful song in a high, loud voice. The strings twanged as he strummed them, not following the rising and falling pitch of his song, but marking time and setting off what seemed to be verses.

The boy carefully avoided looking at Thomas, but when Thomas judged he'd heard enough and began to fish in his pocket for coins, the boy slung the instrument over his shoulder and held out his hand. That was when Thomas noticed the belt that cinched in the boy's khaki shorts. It looked like a broad ceinture fléchée — a finger woven belt worn by country folk in French Canada in the nineteenth century, which was used as a symbol of an independent Quebec during several historic moments.

The belt wouldn't have the same meaning here, but Thomas grinned anyway. It and the boy deserved more than the minimum handout, he thought, so he searched further into his pocket. That morning he'd stowed his US dollars under his shirt in his money belt and all he could come up with was a Canadian dollar coin. "Sorry," he said, "it's all I have."

The boy looked skeptically at the coin.

"Canadian," Thomas said.

The boy looked at him, taking his measure. "Canada," he said. Then he pocketed the coin and turned away.

Thomas was surprised at the irritation that bubbled up unbidden at the way the boy dismissed his money. He'd never had a reaction like that when he'd travelled officially. There had always been smiles and remarks like, "Fine country" and "Number one." Of course, he knew that events then were set up to impress him, but he also expected Canadians to be greeted with some warmth.

He'd have to tell Louise, write it in the journal too. What would she be doing now? Given the time difference — Quebec was eight hours earlier than Bujumbura — she would probably still be sleeping in her little room at the retreat on the Île d'Orléans, lying on her side with the covers brought up close around her face, warm and cozy.

The thought went no further. The blast of the first explosion suddenly overwhelmed the pleasant sounds of breakfast on the terrace. The great thudding noise came from the other side of the hotel compound's walls, but it was so loud that Thomas's ears rang. For a moment, he was paralyzed, unable to imagine what was happening, what should be done. Three of the other men jumped to their feet, while, with great presence of mind, the women pushed the children under the tables and knelt beside them. A baby began to cry. Two uniformed guards who had been walking around the perimeter of the hotel garden rushed through the terrace toward the front of the hotel.

A woman screamed on the other side of the wall, her voice rising in an arpeggio of alarm. A tempest of fear engulfed Thomas and suddenly he found himself blown away from the current crisis, toward that time, months ago, when he last heard a woman scream. It was a sound he had tried to cleanse from his mind.

Wednesday, March 19, 1997
Mile End, Montreal, Quebec
Louise

As she paid the taxi driver, Louise saw Rosa in the living-room window, looking out. Wonderful. It wasn't her usual day to work for Louise, but she had said she might drop by about the time Louise was due home, just to make sure all was well. And there she was, as if she had read Louise's mind. Maybe she'd even bought something for lunch. Louise was starving and she didn't want to have to waste time foraging in the kitchen. The retreat had given her masses of energy and she wanted to get in touch with Frédéric as soon as possible to thank him for the gift he'd given to the retreat. She wanted to hit the ground running.

She smiled at the image as she put the change back in her wallet. She'd never been a runner and now, well, the very prospect left her short of breath. The snow on the ground from a surprise spring storm made the idea of running even more ridiculous. Given the way the plows had pushed knee-high barriers along the sides of the street, she was even going to have a tough time getting up to the door. She would have to climb over it or walk up to the end of the block. The choice was easy to make — she glanced quickly at the driver, who was watching her in the rear-view mirror, and took out more money for a bigger tip. "I'm going to need some help," she said, tapping him on his shoulder lightly. "My days of being a snow princess are over."

He did not laugh at her little joke, but looked at her solemnly as he took the bill she offered. Then, he opened his door and climbed out, pocketing the money as he did. He held the door open for her while she hauled herself out, then reached in to get her suitcase. Offering his arm, he led her toward the packed snow. As she lifted her left foot and tried to plant it solidly, he steadied her, and then, when she couldn't shift her weight upward and forward, he put his hand in the small of her back and pushed. She found herself unsteadily atop the pile of snow for a second before she began to slide down the other side. He reached for her and caught her just before she lost her footing.

No, definitely not a snow princess, she said to herself. "Thank you," she added out loud as she turned to take her suitcase from the driver. She looked up and down the street quickly, hoping that no one had seen her struggle. She felt a familiar panic stir slightly, but her time at the retreat had given her strength to handle this, she told herself. No one but Rosa was watching.

She began to pick her way carefully toward the house. The suitcase wasn't heavy — she'd only been gone four days, and a religious retreat was not a place where you took fancy clothes — but it pulled her off balance, so she lurched as she walked along the snowy sidewalk.

Rosa was still watching from the window when she climbed the front steps. Louise waved and pointed toward the door. "Open it," she said, taking care to say the words clearly so that Rosa would understand by reading her lips. She tried to push from her mind the sudden irritation she felt as she had to wait on the gallery, listening to Rosa coming to the door and unlocking the deadbolt.

"Sorry, sorry," Rosa said, stepping aside so that Louise could enter. "So sorry."

Louise shot a fierce glance at Rosa that the other woman didn't appear to notice, although she was ordinarily alert to things like that. More than once, Louise had found herself comparing Rosa to a watchful rabbit, worried about what would happen next. If Rosa hadn't noticed, something was up, but Louise decided not to ask about it.

"It was marvellous. I wish you had come too," she said, handing Rosa her suitcase and stamping the snow off her boots.

That was not completely true, of course. Louise had indeed asked Rosa to attend this retreat, the way she always urged another parish- | 19 ioner to go with her. She even discreetly underwrote a fund to pay retreat costs so that everyone could pretend that the parishioners from Saint-Michel-de-Mile-End were all simple pilgrims, spending a few days together listening to inspirational speakers and praying in the old house owned by the Fellowship of Saint Laurent on Île d'Orléans. That was a bit of stage-managing though, a way to assuage her conscience over the pleasure she took when no one else could go with her. The Island was so important to her that she hated to share it with anyone.

"It is so beautiful there," she said to Rosa. She didn't bother to take off her boots, but headed down the hall to the kitchen. Rosa followed her. "The storm left about six inches of new snow and then it turned sunny and cold. Just lovely! So brilliant you could hardly stand it. And the ice on the river! Oh I always feel so good after a little time there. And a donation of $80,000 came in — imagine — that means Brother Jean-Marie won't have to sell the building."

She didn't stop at the door to the kitchen, but went on to the garden room, which opened off of it. When she opened the door, the warm, humid smell of growing things flooded out, pushing aside the dry, winter-tempered air of the house. "But winter is winter, and it's good to be back in my little island of summer." She turned around to smile at Rosa. She wanted to lift her out of whatever was dragging her down, to show that you could change things if you tried. That was another thing that wasn't completely true, but long ago she had decided that you had to live your life as if you could.

"There was a message on the answering machine when I got here this morning," Rosa said.

Louise stopped. "You listened to it? Was it from Thomas?" she asked. The people at Witness International, who organized the mission, had said it would be unlikely he'd be able to telephone home. The landlines were limited and passed through Rwanda. Calls still had to be booked in advance. But maybe things were better than they'd foreseen.

Rosa shook her head. "Somebody from Ottawa, I think. I didn't take down the information from the message because I knew you'd be back soon."

Louise quickly shut the door to the garden room and hurried to the phone in the breakfast nook. As she punched in the numbers to retrieve the message, she riffled through the accumulation of papers — mail, faxes from the fax machine. Then the message began and she looked up to smile at Rosa. "If it's from Ottawa, it'll be news from him," she said.

Louise had been nineteen when she met Thomas. He had been twenty-three, and she remembered suddenly, unbidden, but sweet as the little strawberries that grew on the Île d'Orléans in late June, the way he looked when she found herself standing next to him. Frédéric had invited him up to the island — it was Thanksgiving, la Fête de l'Action de grâce — but their family didn't ordinarily celebrate that Anglo holiday. This weekend marked the 300th anniversary of the construction of her family's first house on the long green island that guards the St. Lawrence river downstream from Quebec City. Tom — he was still Tom to everyone then, it would be a while before he came back to his French-Canadian roots and became Thomas — was starting a master's degree in electrical engineering at McGill. He knew Frédéric from his year at Brébeuf in Montreal. Now, Tom and Frédéric had discovered they were living in the same apartment building, and Frédéric obviously thought that Tom would be impressed by the plaque that was going to be unveiled, by the reception that would follow, by the beauty of the island itself.

Louise noticed Tom the minute he came in, but she was supposed to help pass the hors d'oeuvres, and then her mother wanted her to make sure the younger cousins ate their meal properly, without mess. It wasn't until four o'clock, when Frédéric had been captured by their great aunt who was telling him about her health, that she had a chance to seek Tom out. "Let me show you the view of the falls," Louise said to him. "It's not far, and we'll be back before anybody knows we're missing."

Outside, the shadows were creeping over the field, although the hills and the Montmorency Falls across the river still glowed with sunlight. Louise led Thomas along the path that ran from her uncles' house, past the modern bungalow built by the aunt who'd married the shipbuilding money, to the original stone house. Her grandmother and the oldest great aunt lived there, amid a wealth of old and beautiful things the younger members of the family were only occasionally allowed to glimpse. Naturally, the reception was not being held at the uncles' house because it had more room, but because they would not threaten to die if a glass were spilt.

"Three hundred years on the island," Tom said, walking around the stone structure thoughtfully. "My father's family is supposed to have come over about then too, but they certainly had nothing like this."

Louise nodded. She was thoroughly tired of family. She felt suffocated by what her mother was planning for her future — she did not want to teach. The world was changing. Even the Church was changing. But her parents didn't seem to notice. Tom, coming from the States as he did, had a much more direct line to what was happening, she imagined. "Tell me about Boston," she said. "I've never been there."

"Boston," he said, then paused to look at the front door made from a single slab of wood. "Can you imagine the size of the tree that was cut down to get that piece?"

"It was big," she said. She studied him as he stepped forward to tap the door, to look up at the planks forming the ceiling of the porch, to run his hand over the rough surface of the stone walls. He had curly light brown hair. Brown eyes, too. Medium height with broad shoulders, a big head and long arms he swung energetically when he walked. He limped just a bit, his right foot toed in, she noticed, but that was all right. He didn't look like most of Frédéric's friends, which she suspected was a good thing.

"God," he said. "Can you imagine what it must have been like to come here and be able to pick any place you wanted for a house. To say, yes, this is the very best spot."

He had turned to look out at the river. He spread his arms. "To make a whole new world. To set things right."

His words made the fine hair on her arms rise. She shivered, but not because of the chill in the air. She'd sensed a similar excitement with a few of her brothers' *indépendantiste* friends and in the priest who'd taught her ethics class last term, but the energy that Tom promised felt less dangerous than their rage at old forms and old ideas. Afterwards, she decided that was because her body and Thomas's had been suited to each other from the first, making everything else comfortable and almost magically right. Thomas was less angry, less frightening, less driven because, deep in his soul, he assumed that change for the better was possible. The others weren't sure.

"Let me show you something else," she said on an impulse. And she led him through the grass to the hollow.

The hollow was invisible from all of the houses. From the top of the slope, the hillside appeared to be one gradual descent to the river, but for as long as the family had been on the island, children and adolescents had hidden in the hollow beyond the stone wall on hot summer afternoons.

The summer that she was fourteen and Frédéric seventeen, they'd spent a lot of time there, escaping the younger children in the family, the women with their constant tasks and worries, and the boredom of life in the country. They usually took a snack with them, and Frédéric always produced a choice of things to read from his book satchel. Because he and his mother always stayed at the uncles' house, he had access to their large and unconventional library, so several times he brought novels by Balzac and Zola, which were on the Church's Index of forbidden books. He liked to read poetry, too. The week after he'd gone to Montreal to see his father, he produced a slim volume by the poet Paul-Marie Lapointe that he'd found in a used bookstore. And twice he brought poems he'd written himself.

One afternoon, he also had a bottle of wine he'd lifted from their grandfather's cellar. When they reached the hollow, Louise shook out the old car robe that she'd found in their grandmother's garage. Frédéric dropped his book satchel on the ground and took a Swiss Army knife from his pocket.

"My father thought I should have this. It's part of his campaign to make a man of me," he said, as he pulled the corkscrew attachment out of the handle. "He asked if I'd been using it when I saw him, and he was so pleased when I said yes, that I didn't tell him I only use it for opening bottles."

Louise laughed. She never knew when to believe him. There were moments when he reminded her of pictures of saints, with his blue eyes, pale skin and dark hair worn slightly longer than the other boys she knew. She thought she saw an aura of energy surrounding him that she presumed was spiritual. Yet there were other times — like this day when he insisted they bring the stolen wine — when he seemed determined to break the rules.

They'd forgotten the glasses, so once Frédéric had opened the bottle, they each took long drinks from it directly. Their fingers touched when he passed the bottle to her. She looked up into his eyes, hoping to catch him looking at her. But no, he turned abruptly and began searching in his pack for his books.

The air was still, the loudest noise came from the cicadas. Louise's back was against the trunk of an elm, her legs stretched out in front of her. She was hot and wiped the sweat from around her eyes with her fingers while she watched him find the book and reach again for the bottle. "Don't drink it too fast," she said. "It'll go to your head."

"Maybe I want that," he said. He drank from the bottle, put it down, and with a sudden swing of his body, stretched himself out so that he was lying on his back, the book beside him, his head only inches away from Louise's hip.

24 |
He turned his head so he could look up at her. "You ought to try it too." Then after a pause, "Come lay beside me. Come look at the sky with me."

That was exactly the sort of thing she'd been hoping he would say. Of all the boys Louise had encountered to that point, Frédéric was the closest to the one who came to her in dreams, but they were cousins.

But Frédéric did not touch her. Instead, after a moment, he turned over on his belly. "I want you to listen to this," he said, picking the book up so she could see the cover. "You know the story?"

It was *Atala* by Chateaubriand. Louise nodded. They'd read part of it in her French class, the bits about Atala, the beautiful Christian Indian and her immense faith. It was supposed to be uplifting, but Louise had found it boring.

Frédéric watched her face fall. "No, no, it's much better than you think. Just listen. This is when Atala is helping Chactas, the Indian warrior, to escape." And he began to read, "Often during the great heat of the day, we looked for shelter under the moss of the cedars."

As he read, she could see the forest the pair were travelling through, with its vines and wild birds, its rivers and views of distant mountains, and then the threatening storm. As Frédéric read how Chactas held Atala in his arms to shield her from the torrential rain, how he warmed her bare, cold feet in his hands, Louise felt a shiver begin at the base of her spine and radiate outward. She would like Frédéric to warm her feet, she could imagine his fingers sliding up the curve of her instep.

No, this certainly was not what the nuns had them read — the girls had not been assigned the description of ecstasy Chactas felt at Atala's touch, the recounting of how Atala was really the natural daughter of the Spaniard who had taken Chactas in and adopted him. In the excerpt, there had been no mention that in a very real way they were brother and sister. And certainly not, "This fraternal feeling which had come upon us, joining its emotion to our own love, proved too powerful for our hearts ... In an instant I had taken her in my arms, her breath had intoxicated me, and I had drunk all the magic of love from her lips ..." Or, "Atala offered no more than a feeble resistance and I attained a moment of complete happiness ..."

Then Frédéric turned his head to look at her. "Which is where I think I'll stop."

"No," Louise said softly. "No, go on." She was aware of his eyes again, she could not pull hers away from his. "No, please, go on."

But he put the book down and reached over so his hand could encircle her wrist. "Help me," he said. "I need you to help me."

Of course she'd help him. Whatever he wanted. In a second they were laying side by side, their arms around each other. The shrill metallic warning of the cicadas was drowned out by the echo of her heart beating in her ears. She smelled his sweat with its unsettling undertones, whose origins she could not define. She pressed herself against him, she felt her nipples harden and places she was only vaguely aware of grow soft and warm and wet. She wanted something from him that she would have described in the same flowery language that Chateaubriand used because she did not have the courage to speak its true name.

And then he rolled away, lying so his back was to her.

"What's the matter?" she whispered, as if she were afraid they might be overheard.

"I can't," he said. "I can't, not even with you." His voice, so strong and beautiful when he'd been reading, was strangled now. There were tears behind it, she was sure, but only a small plume of fear signalled to her why.

It would be years before she fully understood, although by the time she first stood at the edge of the field with Tom, she knew that she and

Frédéric each had a separate struggle to be the way they were supposed to be.

There had been other young men who came through her life between that particular afternoon with Frédéric and the one with Thomas, but none of them had mattered very much. Starting down the path with Tom, she wondered just where walking with him might lead her over time. This path was too narrow for them to walk side by side, but he didn't let go of her hand, even when she pulled ahead. When they came to the wall, he helped her over. His hand rested on her elbow when they stood, looking down the hillside.

"This is a beautiful place," he said. "Your family is very lucky."

She turned to look up at him and smiled. "You think so?" she asked.

"Yes," he said. "But I don't want to talk about that now." He leaned closer to her. He was whispering, but his words filled Louise's head completely.

She pulled her head back just before his mouth covered hers. His eyes, which had been closing, flicked open. What she saw in them was a longing more intense than she had ever seen. So, she remembered thinking, this is it, this is what it's like. No one else has ever cared as much for me. I would be a fool not to see where this will go.

Back at the uncles' house, with the party rolling on and the family all around, Louise was careful to let Frédéric know where they'd been and, by the hand she kept tucked under Tom's arm, what had transpired.

"The hollow?" Frédéric said. "I haven't been down there in ages. Since that summer we were reading Chateaubriand, remember?" He didn't wait for Louise to reply. He put one hand lightly on Thomas's shoulder. "I was going to take you down there myself tomorrow, my friend," he said. "But now I see that won't be necessary."

He came to their wedding. He was Richard's godfather. He was always, ever after, Louise's very good friend.

But Thomas was her love.

Louise was still awash in memory when a recorded man's voice finally answered her call. She fumed as he said to leave a number because he was away from his desk. She felt like slamming down the receiver after she left her own message, but she restrained herself. Self-restraint — a good quality that her stay at the retreat should have bolstered. For a moment, she sat staring in front of her, thinking first of the peace she had left only hours before, and then slipping back gratefully into memories of Thomas and the Île d'Orléans.

"Would you like something to eat? It's after noon," Rosa interrupted her thoughts.

Louise looked up to see Rosa standing next to the kitchen counter, her hands clasped in front of her, almost as if she were about to pray. It took Louise an instant to return to the present and force a smile. "Food," Louise said. "I'm famished. You don't go on a religious retreat for the cuisine, but I have to say, this time they outdid themselves in lack of inspiration. Dry cereal in the morning, thin soup at lunch and unidentifiable meat for dinner. You didn't get a chance to pick up something interesting for lunch at Ribeira Chà, did you?"

Louise realized she was still wearing her boots and swung her legs around so she could begin to take them off. The space between the table and the chair was tight, and she had to wiggle to get her bulky form free. She was bending over, working at the zipper on her right boot when she heard Rosa make a funny noise.

"No matter. If there are eggs and bacon, we could scramble eggs. Is there bread and butter? I'd love some toast," Louise continued as she struggled with her boot.

Rosa did not reply, and when Louise looked up, triumphant that her boots were finally off, she saw that Rosa had covered her face with her hands and was crying.

"Oh, Rosa," Louise said, "what is the matter? Surely things are not as bad as all that."

But Rosa could only shake her head and sob.

Sunday, March 16, 1997
Hôtel Beauséjour, Bujumbura
Thomas

The second explosion came about five minutes after the first. The noise wasn't as loud, or the blast was farther away, and by then, Thomas was standing with the women and children in the hallway that the hotel's elevators opened onto. "Away from the glass," one of the men had said. "Stay here until we see what's happening."

Théophile stood at the entrance to his office, a light machine gun cradled almost casually in his arm. Thomas couldn't imagine ever carrying a rifle, let alone an automatic weapon, so nonchalantly, but even the most peaceable-looking men here handled firearms.

"Be calm," he found himself repeating as he stood by the elevators. "Be calm and it will be all right." He was holding the hand of a girl who was about eight. With his other hand, he pressed the head of a younger boy against his leg while their mother tried to quiet a screaming baby.

The hotel manager shot a tight smile in his direction. "This is unusual," he said. "There was a bit of trouble last week a little north of town, but we haven't had explosions like this for quite a while."

One of the women said something in Kirundi. The other two women laughed and looked down at their children, pulling them nearer.

"Have you registered with the representative of your country?" Théophile asked. "Madame says you're looking very pale and she wants to know whom we should inform in case you feel indisposed." Then he said something in Kirundi that made all three women and the oldest girl smile. "I just told them that it is winter in your country, which accounts for your pallor. You'll be much better looking after a time in the tropics."

Thomas decided this was something he should laugh at too, but as he did, he wondered about the mention of the need to be registered. Bailey would have seen to that, certainly. The official advice from Canadian Foreign Affairs and the US State Department was not to travel in Burundi, Rwanda or Zaire. Those who disregarded the warnings for whatever reason — and Thomas was sure that only a very good reason would lead anyone to travel to the region — were supposed to make their presence known. For Canadians in Burundi, that meant registering with Oxfam Quebec in Bujumbura because the nearest Canadian consular office was in Rwanda and the nearest embassy in Nairobi. The Americans had an embassy in Bujumbura, and, Bailey said, in a time of crisis, Canadians would be rounded up with Americans and helped to leave the country.

Did this constitute a time of crisis? Probably, but Thomas had no time to worry about that. Two guards from the front of the building rushed through the open breezeway, shouting loudly. Thomas didn't understand what they were saying, but it upset the women and the hotel manager. Théophile shouted back and began herding the group out back onto the terrace.

Thomas followed because he didn't want to be left alone. His heart pounded as they hurried toward the garden and around the pool. The hotel grounds were surrounded by a ten-foot white stucco wall, topped with broken bottles set in concrete, and razor wire strung above that. The wall looked bulky enough to stop most bullets, but

Thomas didn't want to stay out in the open, particularly when the sound of running feet and shouting poured over the wall from outside.

The hotel manager led them to a small building tucked against the wall. It had louvred windows, which were shut, and a padlock on the door. The manager fumbled in his pockets for a key, but when he didn't immediately find it, he took his weapon and quickly shot off the lock. The children began to cry loudly.

30 The building smelled damp inside. Boilers and racks were empty, but from the two washing machines and the mangle along the far wall, it was clear this was the laundry. Down the middle ran a heavy trestle table. "Get under there," Théophile said. "Put the children in the middle. Mesdames, you keep out of sight too." He shut the door behind them and looked around for something to brace it.

In the darkness, Thomas felt the rivulets of sweat on his back run together and begin to course down his spine. He was out of breath after hurrying across the garden, and he knew that he was in no shape for fighting off anyone. He never had been able to run very fast either, since that bout with polio he'd had as a boy.

The manager dragged a chair over to the door and tried to wedge it under the doorknob. "I'm going to have to go back," he said. "There are the other guests and the staff to think of. As soon as I leave, you slip the chair underneath like this."

Sounds of sirens and horns filtered through the shuttered windows, but Thomas heard no gunfire, there had been no more blasts. "Do you think it's really all that serious?" he asked hopefully.

"Who knows?" the manager said. "We don't take chances here."

Thomas had no problem bracing the door after the man left, and then he looked around for a weapon. No one had left behind a firearm, or machete or knife that he could see, but a long iron rod with a hook on the end, used perhaps to open the upper louvres, stood in a corner. It was too long and flexible to be used at close range if it was held by its end, but when Thomas grasped it about halfway down its length, he could wield the hooked end like a club. What damage it could cause remained to be seen — or rather, Thomas hoped he would not have to see. He sat down on the damp concrete floor next to the door with the rod beside him. Two of the children were whimpering, but the women were very quiet. One of the boys crept out from the huddle of children and came over to sit by Thomas. They would not be much of a barrier if anyone tried to storm the laundry, but Thomas was impressed by the boy's spirit.

Thomas had no sense of time passing. The laundry was so dark that the progress of the sun could not even be seen by moving shadows. Two of the younger children had to pee and one of the women crawled to the shelf next to the washing machine, where she found a bucket. Then both the children curled up on the floor and covered their faces with part of their mothers' skirts.

He must have fallen asleep despite the tension because he was suddenly struggling to his feet at the sound of pounding on the door. The women had their hands over the mouth of a child and the boy next to Thomas was on his tiptoes, trying to get an angled look through a small hole in one of the louvred shutters.

Thomas stood up as quietly as he could, grabbing the rod by the middle. He motioned with his head for the boy to get out of the way, and then stationed himself next to the door. His idea was to bring the rod down as hard as he could on the head of whoever succeeded in pushing away the chair blocking the door. The boy saw what he was preparing to do and reached under his shirt to take a long knife from a sheaf, whose outline Thomas had not noticed before. Of course, Thomas realized, these children could have been through this kind of thing before — hiding in sheds and in woods to keep out of the path of killers. Or if they hadn't personally been affected, they knew people who had been rounded up into churches or huts that had then been torched. Or seen the torn bodies of others hacked by machetes. Or, and the thought made Thomas's hand shake as he held the iron rod, they had heard stories told by a loved one of what it felt like to attack another person. Stories told late at night in soft voices when the babies were asleep, when the encircling arms of a beloved could keep away the ghosts. Thomas realized he should not be surprised these handsome women and their well-fed children knew how to behave when killers might be on the other side of the door.

This time, the pounding on the door meant the danger was over.

"Open up," a voice on the other side said. "You can go home now." It sounded a bit familiar, but Thomas glanced over at the women to see if they recognized it. Their cautious expressions did not change. One picked up her toddler and held him close. Two little girls were holding hands, one woman made the sign of the cross.

"Immaculée," another voice said from outside. "I've come back."

"It's my husband and the manager," one of the women said as she began to crawl out from under the table. "Open the door, boy."

The others also struggled to get up, shifting children around, setting the little ones on their feet.

"Now you know what life is like here," the one called Immaculée said to Thomas. "Not like Canada."

"Not like Canada," Thomas repeated as the door opened and the men entered. He stood aside while wives and husbands greeted each other.

He was still holding the iron rod when he and the manager began to walk back across the garden to the hotel terrace. "Going to protect everyone?" Théophile said, pointing to the rod.

Thomas looked at his hand, suddenly surprised at himself. He laughed, "Oh, this." His pulse raced now that he could see just what he had been preparing himself to do. "Don't know that it would have done much good. Where should I put it?"

The manager reached out for it. "I'll take it back when things get straightened around." He paused, as if considering how much to tell Thomas. "The first explosion was an anti-tank bomb at a bus stop up the street, and the second blast was over by the brewery. At least four killed, and a dozen wounded."

Thomas tried to think of what to say, but all that came into his head was the image of the little children covering their faces with their mothers' skirts, followed by the sad face of Sylvain's friend Benjamin after the news of the massacres in Rwanda reached Montreal.

This is Burundi. This is not a memory, this is happening now, he told himself. Up ahead, the families were moving quickly, as if eager to get back home. "Any idea who did it?" he said finally.

The manager looked over at him. "It's complicated," he began, but thought better of it. "I don't know." As they reached the terrace bar, he slipped back into the role of the genial professional host. "Would you like something to eat or drink? We'll be serving dinner at about seven thirty, but perhaps you'd like something before then."

The clock behind the bar showed ten after five. "A soft drink would be good," Thomas said. "I'll take it upstairs and try to nap a little. I'm not used to all this excitement."

He was glad the elevator was working when he started upstairs because he felt wrung out. Once he made it into his room, he went over to the window. Outside, he could see the small hotel across the street, the hills shrouded in clouds, threatening to condense into rain. For the moment, however, a clean blue light flooded into the room. He felt his heart slow and his breathing become more regular. This was light he knew, blue like water at the edge of the Laurentian lakes just after breakup. Only the temperature was different.

Overhead, he saw the first flight of waterfowl heading south, relatively low, as if they were looking for a place to settle on the lake for the night. At home, the geese would also be on the move, going north. Mornings, even in town, he remembered being awakened by the sound of them calling to each other as they took off from the places around the island of Montreal where they'd spent the night. The great Vs of birds would noisily cross the sky, pink with sunrise, and follow the river system north and east. Occasionally, he'd see them in the evening, but not as often.

He passed his hand over his face, rubbed his eyes. For such a long time he'd been too busy in the evenings, although lately, as everybody knew, he had too much time on his hands.

These birds were silent and not flying in formation. Their great wings flapped smoothly through the air, yet not even a breath of their movement was felt on the ground; he heard no rustle of feathers, no questioning call. It was odd that they were flying south. Surely the migration would be north to Europe this time of year, unless the fighting had disturbed their usual nesting spots. More casualties of the conflict. There were so many of them, all flying soundlessly in the same direction. Thomas counted, but lost track after seventy-five. They were moving too fast, the light failing too quickly.

That was the problem, of course. There were so many casualties of conflict.

An amplified call to prayer floated through the window, coming from the west, down the hill, toward the lake. Were there many Muslims here? Louise's contacts had talked as if nearly everyone were Catholic, and as the evening approached on this Sunday, people still passed on the street, heading south, perhaps to the cathedral. Would there be services this late in the day?

He looked at his watch and did the necessary time zone calculation. At this moment Louise might be walking around the island after Mass. It was the beginning of spring, the snow should be melting, the snowdrops would be pushing up through the dead leaves. The air would be sweet as the sleeping earth began to breathe again.

He must call her. He must tell her he is safe because surely she would hear about the attack on the news. But that character who ran the retreat outlawed telephones. He would have to think of another way to make contact with her, to tell her all this and more.

Louise prided herself on being able to comfort people, and she thought she knew Rosa well enough to guess what was bothering her. They'd known each other for years, ever since Louise came across her cowering on a street corner.

Louise had been shopping — the early spring day was so filled with sunshine that she was tempted to go out to buy a few things for dinner. Ordinarily, she ordered by phone from the gourmet grocery on Laurier that specialized in fancy cuts of meat, like racks of lamb and beef tournedos. Thomas was in the Federal Cabinet then, so for more mundane things — toilet paper, laundry soap, frozen orange juice — she commandeered his driver one afternoon a month to take her to the big box store near the freeway. Not only did he help her carry everything into the house, but he was an anchor in the crowded sea of the store. Otherwise, she dreaded shopping.

The day she met Rosa was so lovely that she felt brave. It was time to go out and see what changes had been wrought in the neighbourhood during the winter.

The bagel factory's two storefronts each had lines of people inside waiting to buy, and the owner of the newsstand at Jeanne-Mance and Saint-Viateur — a Greek who always wanted to talk philosophy with Thomas — had pulled a straight-backed chair out onto the sidewalk to sit and smoke a cigarette. Louise nodded as she went by — once she was outside she always nodded when people looked in her direction, which was the extent of her efforts at playing the politician's gracious wife.

It was in coming out of the little grocery store formerly run by an old Orthodox Jew that she literally bumped into Rosa. Louise hadn't been paying attention, she'd been thinking of the changes in the store, which was now called Ribeira Chà. The produce was very nice — she'd bought a pineapple and a small basket of fragrant California strawberries, and she was thinking about the fruit salad with ice cream she'd make for dessert. Marielle, who was currently on a healthy eating kick, would eat the fruit, and the boys could stuff themselves on the ice cream. So could she, she was thinking, when she saw the short, dark-haired woman in her path.

"Sorry, sorry," Louise said, grabbing at the woman before she toppled forward into the street. Louise put her shopping bag down and fought to steady them both. The woman was breathing frantically, Louise saw. Her eyes darted from side to side, looking for an escape.

"Are you all right?" Louise asked, although she could tell something was quite wrong. "Quick, give me your purse and hold your hands up over your mouth and nose so you can breathe into them."

The woman looked frozen, paralyzed by fright. She didn't understand, couldn't act. Louise put her own hand over the woman's face, being careful to cup it a little so she could still breathe. "Now don't be frightened. Just breathe. It's going to be all right."

They must have looked ridiculous, Louise realized afterwards — a big, fat woman in a black cape lined with crimson, wrestling with a shorter, slighter woman in an old ski jacket. Rosa later said that she thought a mad person was trying to suffocate her, but she was too upset to struggle.

"I know what it's like," Louise repeated until Rosa calmed down. "I understand." As they stood on the corner, with passersby giving them a wide berth, she tried to explain how breathing fast makes things worse in a panic attack. "When you're so upset, your body thinks it ought to run, even though it can't. It's waiting for the level of carbon dioxide to rise in your blood because that would mean that you've started to act. So you've got to trick your body by breathing in air you've already breathed out, or by holding your breath." She stopped before she explained more because she suddenly recognized the woman.

"But I know you! You're always at the early Mass at Saint-Michel-de-Mile-End."

Rosa nodded and rubbed her face where Louise had put her hand, but she looked less frightened.

"Where do you live?" Louise asked. "Do you think you can make it home all right? Do you need some help?"

Rosa gestured toward the store. "My husband," she said. "He's in there. I was just going to surprise him. The day is so lovely ..."

"That you thought you could chance it?" Louise said. "Yes, I know just what you were thinking. That nothing bad could happen on a day like this. But then suddenly everything hits you." She looked at Rosa carefully. "I know what it's like," she repeated. "It happens to me too."

Two of the doctors she consulted insisted that the panic attacks must have started before, must go back to a trauma in childhood, but Louise didn't think so. She dated her fear from that awful feature story about Thomas, with its picture of him, Louise and the children back when he was first elected. The picture of them walking on Mont Royal — "Quebec's New Face in Ottawa," said the headline in the *Globe and Mail* — showed her as much heavier than she was. There had been an overheard remark in Thomas's riding office — something about "her majesty, the cow" — and Louise decided she was never going to let herself be exposed again. She would do no public appearances except the inescapable. Over the years, she went out less and less. By the time Sylvain finished high school, it was all she could do to attend the parent-teacher meeting when report cards were handed out. Her contact with the world was mostly by telephone, although there was no doubt that she made herself felt through it. Ordinarily, only things related to God made her venture out in the flesh. Only acts of faith and charity were important enough to risk being ambushed by the world.

"I had a pill," Rosa was saying. "It was supposed to help. I had one left."

"Yes, yes," Louise said. "Let's get you home." She put her arm around Rosa to help her along. "Pills don't help much, you know," she added. She knew this well, but she wasn't going to talk about it now.

Their friendship had grown from there, with their agoraphobia in common, although neither called it by that name. They had their children to talk about too. Rosa's were younger by several years, but each had three — two boys and a girl. They had gone through the same questioning about the Church's teaching on birth control, and decoded — with the counsel of the same young priest who eventually left the priesthood — that it was more important to have all the children you can love than to have all the children you can have.

Then there was the devotion they shared and the comfort they both took in prayer.

The final thing, the one that cemented their relationship, came when Louise told Rosa that she needed help. Her cleaning woman had quit, and "as you can see, I'm in no shape to do it all myself," she had said, holding out her arms to make herself look even rounder. Would Rosa consider coming in three mornings a week?

She did not think about it very long, which did not surprise Louise. The Da Silvas could use the extra money because the Ribeira Chà had begun to founder at that point, and Rosa had already told Louise that she knew she would panic if she tried to help out by ringing-up purchases at the cash register. Working for Louise would be different because Rosa would not have to meet anyone new, and because the walk to Louise's house was so short — only three minutes — that Rosa was still relatively calm when she arrived.

On the negative side of the equation, Louise knew that the employer-employee relation might affect their friendship. The problem had arisen before when another parishioner at Saint-Michel had worked for Thomas as a driver. At that time, Louise had decided that life was too short to worry about it, though. She put herself on guard and willed herself to keep the two relationships separate in her mind. It had worked then, and she intended to do the same with Rosa, because other matters were more important.

39

At the moment, one of them was Rosa and her tears.

Standing in her kitchen, looking at the sorrow written all over Rosa — her body curved forward, her feet turned toward each other, her hands clutching a Kleenex — Louise felt the energy she'd stored up during the retreat drain from her. Even the prospect of news from Thomas couldn't stand up to the worry on Rosa's face.

Louise hoisted herself up and crossed the kitchen in her stocking feet. Her boots had left melting snow on the floor and she shivered as the cold water soaked through. But that was a small thing. "Rosa, what is the problem?" she asked as she put her arms around the other woman.

Rosa shook her head, as if trying to deny whatever was bothering her. The sobs came slower. She twisted away from Louise and blew her nose. "The store," she said when she could speak. "Manny. I don't know, there are such problems ..." Her voice trailed off. She blew her nose again and recommenced. "Manny is a good man, a good husband, a good father. But I don't know. There is something going on."

Louise was not surprised. The last time she had been in the Ribeira Chà — three or four weeks ago, she couldn't remember, because, even though she wanted to encourage them, she still mostly ordered from the gourmet store on Laurier — the lettuce had been squishy with rust, the apples soft and the cheese selection limited to Kraft slices and one big block of orange cheddar. The store had started out well eight years ago. But the neighbourhood was changing, and for whatever reason, Rosa's husband had not been able to adjust.

"Look, I don't want to pry, it's really none of my business," Louise began, because, she always told herself, she truly didn't want to meddle in anyone's affairs. "But are you having financial problems?"

Rosa nodded slowly and took a step away from Louise. She turned so she faced the window that had once opened to the outside, but now separated the kitchen from the garden room. The afternoon sun was no longer shining and Rosa's reflection floated against the darkness on the other side of the glass.

"Has he talked to the bank?" Louise knew about banks. She'd taken over managing their portfolio as soon as Thomas was defeated. As Minister of Industry and Development, he'd tried to avoid the appearance of a conflict of interest, which was much more than many of his colleagues had done, particularly toward the end. They would have been better off after he lost the election if he'd been a little less open and above board, but that was not a subject to think about now.

Rosa was nodding her head again. "He tells me not to worry, you know," she said in a small voice. "He says everything is fine."

"Maybe it is," Louise said, but she doubted it.

They stood there for several moments, Rosa looking into the depths of her reflection and Louise debating if she should ask more. Then Rosa turned abruptly around.

"They smashed the windows last night," she said quickly, as if the words burned her mouth.

"Smashed the windows," Louise repeated. She took a deep breath. Smashed windows, the cold rushing in and Thomas in a fury ... "Who?" she asked, trying hard to control her voice.

Rosa hesitated again before answering, holding her hands in front of her chest as if praying, rubbing them together as if for warmth. "Kids, Manny says. Kids up to no good," she said.

Louise almost hoped so. Kids — young people, teenagers — did bad things but still turned out all right. Look at Sylvain. But she knew — oh she knew, but she shrank from admitting — that others might be responsible for the damage. "What did the police say?" she asked.

Rosa looked away and again hesitated. "He hasn't called them," she said finally. "He says it would make matters worse." She paused and looked directly into Louise's eyes. "That's what really scares me."

Louise pondered that. This was a quiet neighbourhood, people said you didn't have to worry about walking around at night, as far as she knew crime was low. Shadows fell across it nevertheless. The world was full of shadows and she had made it her life's work to keep them at bay. "Do you have insurance?" Louise asked.

It was then that the phone rang. For a moment, neither of them moved to answer it, as the jagged rings cut through the fog of possibilities and fears that had flooded the kitchen. Then Rosa crossed the room quickly and picked up the telephone. She listened for a moment after she said hello. Without saying anything more she handed the receiver to Louise.

"Madame Brossard?" said the man on the end of the line.

"This is she," Louise said, still watching Rosa's face.

"I'm returning your call from the Witness International office," the man said. "Something has come up that I need to talk to you about."

"Please, go ahead," she said. "What is it?" She tried to focus on his words; she tried to remember what she had expected the call would be about.

"Well," he said. "Well, perhaps it would be best to get straight to the matter." He paused and Louise could hear him swallow on the other end of the line. "You're not alone, I gather?"

"No," she said. Smashed windows. She did not like smashed windows.

"Good," he said. "Well, as I was saying, something has come up. Your husband, it seems, well, I don't want to alarm you unduly, but he appears to have gone missing."

Sunday, March 16, 1997
Bujumbura, Burundi
Thomas

When Thomas came downstairs a little after seven, Théophile was busy behind the desk, so he didn't get a chance to ask if there was anymore news about what had happened that afternoon. When the waiter led him into the dining room, he saw that Bailey was already there with the two other observers. Good, Thomas thought. It was Bailey's job to be informed; he ought to know what was going on.

"So you came through unscathed?" Bailey asked as Thomas sat down. Their table was just off the terrace, protected from the rain by sliding glass doors. The wind had flung the rain against the glass, leaving long beaded streaks of water droplets where the glass had been dusty. They refracted the light from the lanterns set around the pool. Thomas's eye caught something moving in the darkness beyond, a man carrying a flashlight perhaps. A watchman. A guard.

To his surprise, Thomas felt himself relax at the idea that the hotel was being patrolled — he had not realized the muscles in his shoulders were so tense. "No problems," he said, and smiled for the first time since the explosion cut short his breakfast. "What about you?" he asked the others, who he hadn't seen all day.

"I was still in my room when it all began," the man from the Mennonite agency said. "Decided to stay there because, if there's one thing I've learned over the years, it's best to stay out of the way when things start exploding."

"That's what I did too," the woman said. She smiled. "It is frequently wise to be wimpy."

| 43

"Words of wisdom," Thomas said, although inside he felt a little pride in the way he had stood guard at the door. Not that he would mention it here.

Bailey ordered beers for all of them and sat back. "What happened was an attempt to assassinate President Buyoya," he began. "There were three bomb blasts at two different locations. The reason you heard the first two so loudly was because they were just around the corner. The third was out by the Amstel brewery. Théophile says to drink up while we can because there may not be much beer coming out of there for a few days. The president wasn't hurt — his car passed just before the first two went off — but it looks like four or five people were killed." He paused. "A terrible business."

No one spoke immediately, each considered what had happened, what might happen, what they had seen elsewhere. Then the woman from the New York office gave a nervous laugh. "Four or five is bad, but it could have been worse. The last time a president of Burundi was killed all hell broke loose."

They all knew what she was talking about. Three years before, almost to the day, persons still unknown shot down a plane carrying the presidents of both Burundi and Rwanda as it landed at Kigali. That started the massacre across the border, where an estimated 800,000 Tutsis and moderate Hutus were killed, most of them hacked to death by machetes in the course of two months. Burundi didn't see the same horrors, but the Hutu-Tutsi conflict had been going on just as long. At that very moment, another former president of Burundi was in hiding at the American Embassy — he'd taken shelter the summer before when he was deposed in a coup led by Buyoya.

"Last week, a lot of rumours about a counter-coup attempt were floating around," Bailey continued. "When I was at the Oxfam Quebec office — that's where I was when the bombs went off, trying to make sure we'll have enough gas for the Jeeps — they were saying that three civilians were arrested on Wednesday on suspicion of plotting to kill Buyoya. Note the word 'civilians.' Now they think the army was involved too because the bombs that went off today weren't homemade ones. They were the kind the military has lots of. Which means there are many forces involved."

He took a drink of his beer, then turned the glass slowly in his hands, looking down into it. No one spoke for a moment. Thomas heard a distant clatter of dishes from the kitchen, the cooing of a bird in the hotel's garden, the murmur of a woman talking softly not too far away.

"So where does that leave us?" The woman from the New York office broke their silence. "I mean, of course we couldn't go any place this afternoon, but we're going to be behind schedule, aren't we?"

Bailey took another sip of his beer. Before he answered, the lights flickered once, and then went out, leaving only the little candles on the tables glowing. The hotel's generator chugged into service and the lights came back on, fainter than before, but still there. "Don't know where they're getting the diesel to run that machine," Bailey said. "Officially, there's been a terrible shortage ever since the embargo began, but you never know what's available on the black market. If it weren't for the hydroelectric projects, most of the country would be without electricity."

He paused again. There were sounds of shouting from the kitchen as a waiter pushed the door open. Thomas found himself looking around anxiously, even though he suspected the noises were normal ones.

Bailey did not react, nor did the others. "But you ask where that leaves us?" Bailey went on. "Well, you knew this wasn't going to be an easy assignment when you took it, right? Ordinarily, we shouldn't let local conditions interfere too much with our mandate. This is probably nothing very serious, nothing that's going to set off anything that would target folks like us." He paused and took another sip of beer. "As long as we have an armed escort we should have no problems. But we'll wait a day just to see how things shake down."

"So what do we do tomorrow?" the other man asked.

"Stick around here," Bailey said. "Study your background documents. Contact any friends you might have at other NGOs." He drained his beer and grinned suddenly. "Christ, you've been around long enough to know the drill. If you don't know how to wait, you're in trouble."

Probably true, Thomas thought. He'd been spoiled. When he was in government, things waited for him. Even back at the beginning, when he'd been one of only three Conservatives from Quebec, the main event never started until he arrived. After the defeat, waiting was one of the things that he had trouble getting used to. Having to look after details was another, and he still didn't handle that very well — when the delegation landed at the great, waterless airport in Nairobi, he didn't look for his suitcase on the luggage carousel because the last time he'd flown his aide had taken care of all that.

The loss. The losses. There were so many things that he missed — the excitement, the women, the feeling that what he did really mattered. A litany of all he missed forced itself on his consciousness, like a spoiled child interrupting a conversation that doesn't concern him. He had to remind himself that he was not here to complain. This trip is not about Thomas Brossard, he told himself for the hundredth time.

But there was one thing.

"Do you think I could send a fax to my wife?" he asked. "She might worry if the assassination attempt makes the news."

Bailey laughed. "That's not likely. What's happening here is pretty

45

much off the radar back home. But if you really want to, it might be possible."

In the morning, Théophile intercepted Thomas as he came out of the elevator. "Monsieur Bailey has asked if you might use the hotel's facsimile machine," he began.

Thomas smiled. Last night, before he went up to his room, he had walked around in the hotel garden. The rain had stopped and the smell of night-blooming flowers lay heavy on the air. From the darkness, he watched an exchange between a man and a woman in the terrace bar, he white, she black. As Thomas finished his drink, he saw how they stood and then began to walk together, his hand on her waist. I want that, Thomas thought, and in his desire he had stumbled over a chaise longue in the darkness by the pool. Someone was laying there, a small man, or a woman wrapped in a shawl, or a tablecloth or a blanket, Thomas couldn't tell exactly. He didn't care, he wanted to do what that man was doing, to stand next to a woman, nuzzling her neck while they waited for the elevator, and then, still breathing in her perfume, go upstairs to his hotel room and take her in his arms.

He didn't, of course. He hadn't done anything like that since the election. But in the night, he dreamed of Louise. Snow and Louise. Her violet velour dressing gown, her flesh. He remembered nothing more than that, but he would have to make do. He was a man who needed dreams when he didn't have a woman next to him.

"But I'm sorry," Théophile was continuing. "Our machine is not working, it hasn't been in operation for a month — it's so hard to get ink and paper — we have to depend on the telephone, which I'm afraid isn't very reliable either."

Thomas nodded. They'd been warned about that after all, although he was surprised to find how disappointed he suddenly felt. Théophile went on, however. "There is a fax machine at the Ministry of Communications, and I've made arrangements there. You'll have to leave the hotel, I'm afraid, but I don't think there is too much danger now. A driver will come for you at about 10 a.m., if that meets your approval."

"Of course, of course." Thomas found himself beaming. "Yes, of course, that would be fine."

Before he sat down to his tea and toast, he went back upstairs to fetch his briefcase so he'd have paper on which to write the message he would send. As he sat on the terrace and emptied the briefcase, looking for writing paper, he found the journal Louise had given him with the edge of an envelope sticking out.

The envelope made him smile.

47

When he first started working for Bell, before he went into politics, he had to travel quite a bit. Not far — Quebec City, Ottawa, now and then Toronto — and never for very long, but Louise tucked little notes into his suitcase. The note might be no more than a line from a song. Other times it was a bit of information she'd forgotten to give him about the house — that she'd called a plumber to deal with the leaking toilet, or that the chimney sweep had come. She included the kids' drawings too, and every once in a while, a photo that he hadn't seen before, a snapshot she'd saved from a roll of film, hiding it so that in his boring hotel room he'd find a new picture of Marielle standing on her head or Sylvain riding his tricycle or Richard with a fish he'd caught. Occasionally, but not often, there were words of love. Then gradually, as he was away more and more regularly, she quit doing it except for birthdays or anniversaries. Now that he was home almost all the time, it had been months since she had surprised him with a note. Certainly not since the incident with the violets.

So this envelope pleased him even before he opened it. It wasn't large — the standard business-letter size — but thick enough to suggest it contained several sheets of paper. He picked it up and slipped his index finger underneath the flap, tearing the paper a little in his haste. He searched for a note from her, but found only a few words written at the top of a photocopied page: "Maybe this will come in handy."

Not all that promising, he thought. But he smoothed the pages, which had been folded in thirds, so that he could see more clearly. The photo of a young African woman, bedecked in many necklaces, with a shaved head and high cheekbones anchored the corner of the page. *National Geographic*, November 1962, "Freedom's Progress South of Sahara," it read.

Thomas laughed out loud. When Monsieur Desjardins, Louise's father, took on clearing out the basement of their big old house in Outremont as his first post-retirement job, Louise claimed the collection of *National Geographics* that had been accumulating since she was a girl.

48|

"All right, you get points for that," he said aloud as he looked more closely at the article. It began with the author saying that he'd arrived in Ruanda-Urundi, the territory administered by Belgium since 1916, on the eve of independence.

"In June, fear scented the air of Usumbura, the capital, just as surely as did the heavy sweetness of the frangipani that lined its streets. Belgian troops were scheduled to begin their departure on July 1, when the two independent states — the Republic of Rwanda and the Kingdom of Burundi — would emerge. Of the 8,000 Europeans who were living in Ruanda-Urundi, more than half had fled from the Congo — and they remembered."

Even then, Thomas read, the two little countries had the highest population density in Africa and the Hutus and Tutsis were massacring each other. There were pictures of men with loads on their heads, walking barefoot down the hills toward town, past the buildings of the "ultramodern school" of the Collège du Saint-Esprit, as well as a photo of a crowd of traditionally dressed worshippers in the Jesuit school's chapel.

Usumbura, the capital. Usumbura, like that other name for African violets, *les violettes d'Usumbura*, Thomas thought. The town must have become Bujumbura at some point, probably because of the prefixes that the language here attached to words — Tutsi and Hutu weren't really the proper names one of the background papers said. Batutsi or Bahutu is the name of an individual member of the groups, while the groups themselves were the Wahutu and the Watutsi.

Watutsi, Watusi: wasn't that the name of a dance? Another memory flash, and he was standing near the entrance to the gym at UMass, one of those mixer dances, stressful for most people, an agony for a young man who knew his legs would not, could not dance. "The Wah Watusi," that was the title and the group was from Philadelphia, American Bandstand country. All those clean cut middle-class kids gyrating to music which was linked, although they did not know it, to another reality half way around the world. How strange, how strange.

Louise, his Loulou, who didn't mind his imperfections, who never said anything about dancing once he told her why he couldn't.

It had been late winter the first time he went to her parent's house for dinner, a Sunday in February. She said she'd meet him at the bus stop on the corner of Park Avenue and Laurier. He dug out the one dress shirt that remained clean and ironed from the half-dozen his mother had packed for him before he left for Montreal. He shaved closely. He brushed his teeth twice. Even though it was so cold the snow squeaked under foot, he decided not to wear a toque because the knitted cap flattened his hair and made him look stupid, he thought.

As the bus ran along the eastern edge of Mont Royal from the downtown neighbourhood near McGill where he lived, he began to wonder if he were making a mistake. So far, he'd avoided anything like this with the parents of girls he'd gone out with. Most of them had been in flight from their comfortable suburbs, so they had no desire for cozy meetings around a dinner table anyway. The nearest thing had been an embarrassing evening drinking beer in Amherst with a girl he'd dated at UMass and her father, who was half-loaded already when they started.

This was not likely to be anything similar, and Thomas wasn't sure if that were good or bad. As the bus made its way up Park Avenue, past the four-storey apartment blocks with stores on the ground floor, he

49

wondered what would happen if he just stayed on the bus. He'd never taken it to the end of the line, up somewhere near the east-west freeway. Maybe he should just stay on and take the bus back downtown. Avoid the whole exercise completely. Pretend he was confused about the date. Light out for the territory, like Huck Finn.

He couldn't keep himself from looking out the window, and he saw Louise standing on the corner of Laurier, her face pretty and plump and pink, her hands stuck in the pockets of her duffle coat, her silly little red hat pulled down on one side so that she looked like a newsboy from a silent movie. Even from a distance, he could see the way her breath was making clouds in the cold air, and he felt a sudden tenderness for such sweetness waiting for him despite the winter weather, for a girl who knew a few of his secrets — if not all — yet still wanted to be around him. No other girl had put up with temperatures twenty degrees below freezing in order to meet him, no one else had a smile that lit up in quite that way when she saw him getting off the bus.

He found himself opening his arms to her and kissing her quickly on the mouth, right there on the street corner, with people walking briskly around them on their way to their own Sunday pleasures. He was lost, quite lost, he knew then. Whatever her family was like, he wanted her on whatever terms she would set. He put his arm around her as they walked, and she matched her step to his so well that his limp did not interfere.

If he had calculated, if he had had an inkling of what his future might hold, he wouldn't have been able to find a better family with which to ally himself. "You'll like them," Louise said when he stopped just before the walkway leading to the house, with its broad gallery in front and its stained glass windows, its expanse of snow-covered lawn and its three cars in the driveway. "And they'll like you." She smiled at him. "I promise you." Then she leaned forward quickly and kissed him again on the cheek.

Louise's two brothers were there, the older one with his pregnant wife, the younger one with his fiancée. Madame Desjardins appeared, carrying her youngest grandchild, followed by Louise's sister, leading her little boy by the hand. The brother-in-law took Thomas's coat. Maître Desjardins came down the stairs, holding out his hand for Thomas to shake. Everyone did indeed seem pleased to meet him.

Their questions were polite. That his parents were both from families with their roots in the Beauce river valley was of interest to everyone, although Thomas had no idea if he was related to the Brossards of Saint-George-de-Beauce or to those of Beauceville. His French was complimented, although he knew just how terrible his accent was — the year *en pension* at Brébeuf had steeled him to teasing about that. His choice of McGill for engineering was discussed in relation to the two years Louise's brother spent there doing a master's in psychology. His father's GI-bill education was compared to the Canadian programs for veterans. He was confused by what fork to use, and at first had no idea what the knife bars were for, but no one commented, no one even seemed to notice. He was told not to help clear the table. He was asked if he would like a game of billiards in the basement with the men.

Yet, he had enough presence of mind to realize that despite the thin china painted with violets and the battery of heavy silverware, this was a family where it was not a virtue to be idle, where Madame was proud of her tarts, pork roast and flower arrangements, and of being *une bonne ménagère*. There was a maid, Louise told him later, but she had Sunday off after ten thirty, which was early enough for her to go to the 11 a.m. Mass, but late enough so that she could peel potatoes and carrots beforehand. The women of the family did the clearing up after dinner, and the men were expected to stay out of the way.

"So you're here on a student visa?" Louise's older brother asked after they'd all chalked-up and the brother-in-law broke.

Thomas nodded. Certainly he had let Louise understand that he had come to McGill to do his master's in electrical engineering largely because he was disenchanted with Vietnam. She smiled at that, it went with the kind of sweet religion she believed in, as well as a snobby disdain for many, but not all, things American. It was true he didn't think much of the war the US was involved in, but he didn't know what tack he should take with her parents. Her father, after all, had been in the French-Canadian regiment, the Royal 22nd, the Van Doos. But it was Thomas's turn to play, so no one remarked that he didn't elaborate.

He shot poorly, with the ball skittering inches right of where he aimed. He gladly made way for Louise's youngest brother.

"But the draft hasn't become an issue for you?" the brother-in-law asked.

"Not yet," he said. "It might," he added, still watching the play. The brother was very good.

"Because of Vietnam?" Louise's father asked.

The balls clicked against each other as the brother shot, then thudded solidly into the pocket. Thomas knew he had to reply honestly if he were to hope to spend much time in this family. "Because of Vietnam, mostly," he said. "Because of the war the US has got itself into, but also," he added when the turn had passed to Louise's other brother, "because I can't see myself slogging through swamps. I don't want to die in the jungle. I'm not a hot weather man."

"*Tiens, tiens,*" the brother-in-law said. "Not a hot weather man. Well, this is the right season for you to come to Montreal."

Yet here he was in Bujumbura. He opened the journal and began to write a message to Louise on the first page.

He had rejected four starts before finally finding the words that might say what he wanted to say, when Théophile came around the corner from the reception area. He was accompanied by a tall black man, whose black hair was sprinkled with white. The man's frame was thick through the shoulders and gut, as if he'd been growing older in circumstances that allowed him good food and drink and not a lot of exercise to work it off.

Thomas tore his finished letter from the journal and stood up, trying to figure out where the man fit in. He was wearing pressed dark trousers and a blue long-sleeved dress shirt with the cuffs rolled up. His glasses had metal frames almost exactly like those Thomas wore himself. He definitely wasn't an ordinary driver. Perhaps a businessman, a government official, a military officer in civilian clothes?

"My good friend Bonaventure Nzosaba, who will be your guide," Théophile said. "A man who knows the city as well as anyone."

"At your service," Nzosaba said, putting out his hand to shake Thomas's. In his other hand he held a small piece of paper, which he waved at Thomas. "I have instructions. Shall we go see if we can get your message sent?"

"I will tell Mr. Bailey that you've left," Théophile said, "and that you are in good company."

Thomas saw no reason to object. He stuffed his papers back in his briefcase, picked it up and turned to follow Nzosaba. As soon as he crossed the reception area, he could see the white pickup truck with "Les Industries Nzosaba" painted on the door parked just outside. A young man in uniform already sat in the back, an AK–47 cradled on his knees. Nzosaba held the door on the passenger's side open for Thomas, then handed him an umbrella to hold. "There will be rain before long," the man said. "Better be prepared."

Thomas smiled. "For all eventualities."

This morning there was only one other vehicle in the parking lot, a white SUV with a UN logo on the side. Two armed guards stood on either side of the driveway, and just outside the gate, a group of men squatted and leaned against the wall that separated the hotel's property from the street. When their vehicle drove up, the guards waved them through and then turned toward the loungers, with their hands on their weapons. It seemed to Thomas to be a menace that had become ordinary with repetition.

Nzosaba headed south toward the traffic circle next to a park.

A honking truck cut in front of them. It was the kind with an open back framed in metal bars in which people, as well as goods, could be transported. This one was full of young men in uniform, even though there seemed to be no official insignia on the vehicle. Nzosaba had to swerve out of the way.

"Soldiers?" Thomas asked once they were safely past.

"Militia. Things are still unsettled," Nzosaba said. "But don't worry, we'll take good care of you." At the first intersection after the *rond point*, he had to slow because the sidewalks were overflowing with pedestrians. "See? People are coming from the suburbs to buy and to sell. The market is nearby," he said.

54

Thomas nodded. Markets had been standard places to visit when he was heading official delegations. Things were always cleaned up for the Canadians, he knew, and he'd become used to being presented with a bouquet of flowers by a little girl whose mother or grandmother had a stall at the market. He took it as a given that markets were rarely as photogenic when visiting politicians were absent.

Nzosaba turned right onto a street bordering the market space. Honking at the pedestrians who surrounded the car, he slowly drove through the crowd. The windows were down, and Thomas could make out the smells of dried fish, spices and chickens. The mix was not unpleasant — despite the heat, despite the turmoil, the stench of rotting flesh and sewage was notably absent. By afternoon, he imagined, the place would be less inviting.

"It's not much farther to the office where you can send your fax," Nzosaba said, turning to smile encouragingly at Thomas.

"Are there more people than usual?" Thomas asked. Every inch of the covered space that he could see from the vehicle appeared to be filled with either merchants and their wares, or people bent on buying.

"Actually, this is after the biggest crush. The curfew is lifted at sunrise, and people start arriving as soon after as they can. Probably most of the ones who are here now have had to come a longer distance," Nzosaba said. "Given the circumstances, there may actually be fewer of them than usual. Things have been very dangerous in the hills."

Thomas said nothing, but continued to look. His white face was obviously remarked, as several men stopped and stared back at him.

The women didn't, perhaps because they did not stand tall enough to meet him eye to eye as he sat in the pickup, or perhaps because they were too busy with the baskets they had balanced on their heads.

The background papers said that Tutsis made up the vast majority of the population of the city of Bujumbura, so Thomas tried to determine just who among the people surrounding the pickup were Hutu.

A half-dozen men stood much taller than the others headed toward the market, Thomas saw. They were lean, with high foreheads and relatively thin faces. The rest of the men and women were several inches shorter, with most of the women selling things wearing brightly coloured pieces of cloth tied around their waists to form a skirt. Another length of fabric with a matching design covered their shoulders, and often a third was tied around their heads. Those with bare heads either had their hair braided in small sections, or cut short in a style that must have inspired the Afro in North America. A few women among the shoppers had their hair braided too, but with extensions so that the tiny plaits formed designs on their scalps and then fell into bunches of complex braids. Two women dressed in skirts and blouses had smoothly processed hair. They were accompanied, Thomas saw, by short men in shorts and T-shirts carrying baskets — ladies and their servants.

One of the women with plaited hair straightened after examining a pile of mangos at a stall just inside the market. As she did, her eyes met Thomas's. Her face was unsmiling, but she allowed her gaze to remain on him. Her skin was chocolate brown and smooth, and her body, in its short-sleeved, raspberry coloured dress, rounded. Beautiful enough to make you eat your heart out, Thomas thought.

Nzosaba saw who Thomas was looking at. He frowned slightly, as if disapproving. Thomas noticed and quickly tried to think of a question to get away from the delicate territory of relations between men and women. "Is there much of a textile or garment industry here?" Thomas asked. Textiles, garments, tea, coffee — they were always good for conversation in a third world country.

The other man decided to go along with the tactic. "We don't have anything to make textiles with," he began. A little cotton was grown, but not enough to make an industry. All petroleum was imported, the logistics of transport complicated — in short, a litany of problems that lasted long enough to get them past the market and down the street to the office where Thomas was to use the fax.

The building had just been completed and scaffolding still clung to its sides, while piles of sand for cement sprawled beside the planks set out as a walkway from the street to the entrance steps. Nzosaba led the way and Thomas tried to follow quickly, bouncing along to keep his feet from twisting as the boards moved underfoot. Two armed guards — or perhaps these were soldiers? — stood on either side of the open doors. Their own young escort stayed with the pickup and his AK–47.

Nzosaba showed the guards his identification and explained in Kirundi why they were there. Thomas put on his serious, interested expression, the one he'd perfected as camouflage during a thousand briefings when he wasn't quite sure what was happening. The older guard motioned them inside, smiling at Thomas and saying, "*Bonjour,*" as he passed.

The office they headed for was to the right, while the post office and post boxes were on the left. Nzosaba led Thomas to the line of chairs facing the reception desk. Thomas saw the telephone, two computers and a few other office machines beyond the desk. "It'll take a minute," Nzosaba said, before going over to shake hands with a woman at the desk and the two men who were talking to her.

As Thomas watched, any doubt that Nzosaba was an ordinary guide dissolved. From the deference the others showed him, he was obviously well-known and a person to whom people paid attention. This raised the question of why he was showing Thomas around. Possibly because the hotel management considered it important to stay on the good side of the observation team and had enlisted the help of a well-placed friend. Possibly because the manager, or a government official or Nzosaba himself had looked into Thomas's background and decided that it might be useful to befriend a man who had once been powerful and who might still have powerful friends. Almost certainly someone expected to get something out of being nice to Thomas. That was the way things worked in most places — no, all places — Thomas believed. But before he could consider what these people might want, he saw Nzosaba suddenly stand straighter after hearing what the woman was saying. All four of them at the reception desk cast quick glances at Thomas, and then spoke heatedly among themselves in carefully quiet voices.

The woman picked up the receiver on her telephone and dialed, while Nzosaba leaned forward, both his hands on the edge of her desk, his face about two feet from her's. The two other men consulted the papers in their hands, but paused and looked up when the woman handed the receiver to Nzosaba.

"Promise ... Canada ... yesterday." Thomas picked out a handful of words from the stream that Nzosaba yelled into the telephone. But then he smiled and nodded. He looked over at Thomas and motioned to him to come closer.

"Sometimes, you have to argue a bit," he said when he put down the receiver. "Bureaucrats," he added.

"They're like that all over the world," Thomas said. "I take it that it can be difficult to get clearance?"

Nzosaba nodded again and put his hand on Thomas's back to guide him out of the office. "Do you have the message ready to go? Good," he said when Thomas opened his briefcase and pulled out the sheet of paper with the final version of his message to Louise. "You've noted down the number? Fine, I'll only be a minute. You wait here."

Wait here. The kind of thing that you'd hear in offices everywhere. It always made Thomas impatient. The only time cabinet ministers wait is for the prime minister or for extremely generous donors. Certainly, there were other people waiting here. It even looked as if the people working there were waiting. For what?

Then he heard the telltale chirping of a computer making an internet connection and saw a map on the wall with lines that might be transmission lines.

Transmission lines. Bailey had mentioned problems stemming from the lack of telephone land lines and the importance of radio as a means of communication all over the African Great Lakes region. Governments, political parties, even NGOs had their own radio stations. The bloodbath in Rwanda had been started by a call to action on the radio.

Bloodbath. What had happened in Burundi in 1972, 1983 and 1993 was not as terrible as Rwanda in 1994, but the carnage over the years had been enormous — hundreds of thousands was a low estimate. Yet the group of people working in this office hardly looked like human beings who could be swept up in mass destruction. That tall young man with the red tie, grinning to himself as he read a letter from the sheaf of papers he held in his hand, the older man with the light blue shirt and the perfectly tailored dark blue jacket, the pretty young woman with her hair looped into hoops behind her ears and her red flowered dress — none of them looked to be capable of evil, nor to have been touched by it. And that, Thomas realized, was the most disquieting thought he'd had since he stepped off the plane.

Nzosaba returned, holding out Thomas's message. "No problem, went through the first time. I didn't ask for a confirmation of reception — it's too early for anyone to be at work in Montreal, I imagine."

Thomas looked at his watch and did the calculation. "Yes, it's still long before sunrise, but it's not an office actually, it's my home, and my wife is away on a religious retreat," he said.

Nzosaba looked at his own watch, then glanced at Thomas, as if considering. Thomas wondered if he were calculating what sort of person would have a fax at home in Montreal, or what kind of people went on retreats there.

"Well in that case, you'll be interested in visiting the cathedral," Nzosaba said. "It is not far, and my friends here say that the city remains calm."

To explain that he was not religious would only confuse things, Thomas decided. "Whatever you think I ought to see," he said, following Nzosaba out to the street. Well, why not? He'd already decided that Louise would like a report on it. Besides, waiting in the hotel this afternoon would be boring, and if any place were safe, you'd think it would be the cathedral.

The armed guard stood beside their vehicle, his weapon slung on his back. He was skinny, and younger than Thomas thought at first, a boy really. Nzosaba went around to the driver's side, saying something in Kirundi that led the guard to first open the door for Thomas and then jump in the back himself.

They headed down a paved street with low buildings on either side, mango and frangipani trees hanging over walls from protected gardens. Not a residential neighbourhood as such, but quite different from the commercial section they'd been in. At the end of the road loomed the cathedral, which, to judge from the style of architecture, must have been built in the 1950s or 1960s, about the time of Independence or just before. Faced in yellow tile with three tall, narrow-arched windows across its front, the building looked like a testament to the grand, modern future that appeared possible when it was built. A bell tower at one side rose twice the height of the building, which itself was about as high as a four-storey office structure. Inside, the space soared, drawing your eyes — and perhaps your prayers — upwards, as in a Gothic church. Thomas wondered what Louise's cousin would say. When Thomas was in office, Frédéric regularly ranted about how the federal government should require more imaginative architecture in the buildings it commissioned. "The National Arts Centre, fine, Safdie did a nice job, but the rest ... my God, what disasters," Thomas could hear him saying. "You need authentic architecture, you need buildings that reflect the climate and the light," Frédéric insisted.

Did this building do that? Certainly Nzosaba seemed proud of it. "You should see it on Sunday," he said as they walked up the concrete steps onto the covered porch, where worshippers who couldn't crowd inside might take shelter when it rained. Their guard followed them, but stopped when they reached the doors. Perhaps things had not deteriorated to the point where it was considered permissible to carry firearms into churches. He remembered the hundreds of Tutsis who had taken sanctuary in Rwandan churches and had still been slaughtered. But Nzosaba was continuing — "The church is packed for each Mass, you can't get in the door."

The day had begun to get quite warm, yet inside the sanctuary Thomas felt a cool dampness lingering from the night. A priest was saying Mass at the altar, with about two-dozen people clustered in the front pews. It was hard to tell what age they were from the back, but only a couple appeared to be old women like those who attend Mass at Louise's church on a weekday morning.

The priest held out his arms and said a benediction, although Thomas did not understand the words. The congregation mumbled a reply. The service was over. Two women, both in dresses and wearing lacy scarves on their heads, began to exchange a few words with another woman in the pew behind them. A tall, heavy man with greying hair pulled himself stiffly to his feet and started to make his way slowly toward the door. He was dressed in a white short-sleeved dress shirt, and carried over his arm a jacket that matched his trousers.

Nzosaba was saying — "There has been some difference of opinion between the government and the Church, but as you can see, people even come to pray during the week." He gestured toward the front of the church, "Would you like to take a closer look?"

"My wife would never forgive me if I didn't," Thomas said. As they walked down the aisle on the left side of the church, he saw a little girl. She apparently had been near the front, waiting until the end of the Mass. She scurried to the end of the aisle where she could talk to people as they left. A smaller boy followed her, taking hold of the skirt of her dark red velvet dress. She stationed herself so that no one could avoid her. The boy's shirt was crisply pressed and his navy blue shorts looked clean, but both of them were barefoot, and neither carried anything.

Marielle had a fancy dress like that for parties when she was about six, Thomas remembered. She was his sweetheart then, his little dolly, climbing up on his lap after dinner, pushing the boys away. Louise made noises about Freudian attachments at that age and smiled. She could do nothing else, he figured, because she had been her Papa's darling too. Marielle loved the dress and wore it for every possible occasion. She'd finally split the seams bending over to pick up a present the Christmas she'd definitively outgrown it. She rarely wore skirts now, she preferred jeans when she wasn't wearing hospital scrubs, but she'd been so cute prancing around in that dress.

This little girl wasn't begging exactly, she seemed merely to be asking if she could tell her story. Her voice had a cheerful tone to it, although Thomas could not make out what she was saying. As Nzosaba continued toward the front of the church, Thomas stopped to listen, to watch her smile light up when she began talking to the parishioners. No one answered her, and after each attempt, the girl's smile dimmed for just a second before starting toward her next target. The boy followed behind, his face never changing from its serious, watchful expression.

The girl saw Thomas and hesitated a moment. White faces were not unknown here — some of the priests were white. Either she was unused to approaching white people, or she needed to consider what strategy would work best. She danced over to him, stopped, and reached out to touch his hand, her eyes big and black. She was smiling, asking him something. "School uniforms," he thought she said in French, the accent quite different from the one he was used to. Yes, "school uniforms," and "pencil."

Nzosaba materialized beside him, speaking directly at the girl in Kirundi. He flapped his hands at her, palms outward, shooing her off. The girl looked puzzled for a moment, but put her hand up to her mouth, as if to stifle a giggle. Her eyes snapped at Thomas, daring him to react, inviting him to join her in a game that she was sure he'd enjoy.

"No," Nzosaba said loudly in French so Thomas could understand. "The gentleman does not want to be bothered. Who gave you permission to beg in here? Why are you not in school today?"

The girl began chattering so fast that Thomas wouldn't have understood even if she had been speaking French. She pointed in the direction of the entrance through which the priest had left. Then she pointed toward the outside with her other arm, including the little boy in her gesture. He stared straight ahead, stoically, as if he were used to such questioning, and knew that nothing he could do would change the inevitable outcome.

"No," Nzosaba repeated. He put a hand on Thomas's arm to restrain him from taking change from his pocket. "Run along," he said. "You shouldn't be doing this." He shifted his touch to a grip on Thomas's elbow. "We have stayed here long enough," he said.

The noontime light was bright outside, the asphalt of the street burned in the sun. Thomas stood blinking for a moment on the church steps, getting his bearings. Their guard, who had been talking to another armed man beside a Land Rover, quickly straightened up when he saw them. A group of boys in khaki shorts and white shirts trooped past, talking loudly, satchels like those of European schoolchildren on their backs, going home from morning classes.

"We will not talk of that child," Nzosaba said. "But tell me, would you like to see more of the city?"

62

Louise set the telephone down and shut her eyes, remembering the long discussions they had before Thomas agreed to go on the mission. They had both said that in an ideal world Louise would go to Burundi.

"He's gone missing," she said to Rosa. "They don't know where he is. He went off ..." Her voice broke. She put her hands up to her face. Her thoughts spun around and around, sending off sparks that did nothing to illuminate the darkness she felt settling around her. This was not supposed to happen. This was a trip to help him, not harm him. She'd worked so hard to set it up, at persuading the people at Witness International that they needed Thomas and his expertise.

Rosa wiped her own tears from her face and stared at Louise, as if she were having trouble registering what Louise was saying. She stepped toward Louise, ready to embrace her, to offer comfort the way Louise always had for her.

But Louise turned out of Rosa's arms, taking a step backwards, grabbing hold of the countertop. "No." She stood up straight and attempted to square her shoulders. "It will be all right," she said. "Everything will be all right."

She had almost lost him more than once before. The first time was back at the beginning, when he received his draft notice that his mother had forwarded from Boston. He pulled it from his mailbox on a night in July when she had come over to fix him dinner. His place was at the back of the building, with its two windows facing west on either side of the fire escape. Both were always shut and locked, even in the summer heat, to keep out thieves — the neighbourhood was a little dangerous.

Louise knew the place would be stifling. She had bought lettuce, tomatoes, canned shrimp and a loaf of crusty bread for dinner because it was too hot to think of cooking in even a well-ventilated place, let alone his hole. But she was glad to be there, and pulled him upstairs before he had a chance to look at his letters. The stairwell smelled of rotting garbage from the overflowing bin at the bottom of the landing. A wave of hot air rushed out when Thomas opened his door, but at least it didn't smell.

"So," she said when she had opened the windows and turned on the fan. He was standing by the table he used both to eat and study on. In one hand he held the flyers that had made up most of the mail, in the other he had a letter that he was reading with great intensity. "So," she repeated, "what's up?"

"I'm supposed to report for a physical in Boston." He looked at her. "I thought I'd be safe."

She looked from his face to the letter. "What are you talking about?" she asked, reaching for the paper.

"No," he said. "Damn it, I told you about this. Vietnam. It's just that I thought my number was good enough to get me through."

The Americans had switched to a draft lottery — last winter, every nineteen-year-old male was classed by his birth date. Because Thomas had had a student deferment, he was included, even though he was twenty-three. "But you said they'd never get around to you — what were you, number 200?" she asked.

"No. 195, don't you remember anything? Oh shit, shit, shit." His voice was loud, his face red, he was as upset as she had ever seen him.

She put her arms around his waist and leaned against his back. His shirt back was wet with sweat, and his smell — a mixture of deodorant soap and young man — filled her head. She'd made her choice already. The afternoon last fall on the Île d'Orléans had been the beginning, but the winter had confirmed it. She was sure he felt the same, it was just a matter of time.

"Why don't we just get married?" she asked, the words floating out of her mouth like little puffs of happiness. She didn't stop to consider them, she forged ahead, sure she was offering him the perfect solution.

In her daydreams he would joyously enfold her in his arms at this point, but instead, his body froze, his breathing stopped. He pushed her arms away and took a step back.

"No, you don't understand, that won't help. That won't help at all. Getting married won't give me a deferment. The whole point of the lottery is to get away from deferments — for students, teachers, for married men, for everybody." He turned toward the window and looked out at the heat rising in waves off the roof next door. "The only hope would be if they classified me 4-F, gave me a medical deferment because of my leg."

She knew what 4-F was, he'd mentioned it before — all that business about having polio as a kid. "Don't worry about that," she said, "don't worry about being 4-F or whatever. You could stay here if we got married." She'd thought it through already. "You could immigrate. There'd be no questions asked," she said. "The fast track."

He was not paying attention. "4-F because of my leg," he repeated. "But it's chancy; the bastards are just as likely to say that the limp hasn't bothered me since I was a kid ..."

"Getting married would be much, much easier," she continued, paying him no mind. She stepped closer to him, touched his shoulder, hoping that would help convince him. She put her cheek against his back and wrapped her right arm around his chest again so she could finger his shirt buttons. "Besides, like I've told you, you're silly to dwell on your leg. It's nothing," she said.

Saying that was a mistake. She knew as soon as the words were out of her mouth, she felt his body grow absolutely rigid. "Nothing?" he said. "How do you know?" The paralysis of anger gave way to active fury. He whirled around without looking at her. In two steps he had opened the door and was running down the stairs. She heard him crash into the garbage bin at the bottom and open the front door. She reached the window just in time to see him running along the street, headed somewhere, anywhere.

Her first thought was a little bubble of satisfaction that his limp didn't seem to bother him at all. That night last winter, when he'd explained about having polio, he had been so worried that she wouldn't understand, that she might even be repulsed. She loved him anyway, she told him, she didn't care at all that his left leg was a little shorter than his right. He'd been so pleased, as if he'd feared that imperfection was so heavy it would weigh him down forever. "See," she wanted to tell him now, "you were making a big thing out of nothing."

Her second thought was that maybe she ought to run after him despite the heat, despite the fact that even then she was no athlete. But her third thought was the realization that she really didn't have to worry because he would come back. He had to, it was his apartment. But more importantly, he was like that. He came back. If she waited, he would always return — it became the rock on which their partnership was built.

Two days later, she told her father that she would not join the family on the Île d'Orléans that weekend. It was another hot day, a Friday, and they were sitting on the gallery in the back of their house

66 |

in Outremont. Her father had a whisky-soda next to him on the little wicker table and was working his way through the stack of newspapers that he hadn't had a chance to read during the week.

"Maman thinks I'm coming with you tomorrow," Louise said. "I tried to talk to her on the phone about it, but all she wanted to do was give me a list of things to bring. You'd think you couldn't buy anything at all on the island."

Her father laughed. "Well you can, but you have to pay a price for them. Your mother is just being practical. An excellent quality. I hope you're taking notes so you'll be as good a wife as she is."

"Wife," Louise repeated. She took a deep breath and leaped into her future. "That's just it. I'm getting married. To Thomas. Next week."

He looked at her over the rim of his glass. She was sure she was his favourite. She was the youngest by six years, and he'd always stood up for her when the older ones teased her. She received the dolls that she wanted from the Eaton's catalogue, and even the little bunny-fur cape that she saw in the window at Dupuis Frères that her mother said was far too expensive and impractical for a child of her age. Her sister sulked both times, but her father only said that teenagers shouldn't resent the littlest ones, who had to put up with abuse from all the older ones.

He put the paper down on his lap and reached for his drink. "You want to get married," he said. "To that American fellow. Next week." A nighthawk buzzed through the twilight, and tennis balls could be heard plopping gently back and forth in the tennis courts on the next street.

She looked at him and nodded.

"So suddenly," he said, as if to himself. He coughed and cleared his throat. She knew what he was thinking, she was hoping he'd be too embarrassed to ask. He coughed again. "You haven't told your mother? You haven't confided in your sister?"

Again she shook her head no.

One of the things she had figured out when she was about thirteen was that her sister must have been conceived on their parents' wedding

67

night. There were nine months to the day between their anniversary, May 26, and the birth of their first child, February 26 of the next year. There was a family joke that her mother had spent the last two months in bed so she would not deliver early. Babies born too soon were a touchy topic in the family.

"Next week," he repeated. He considered a minute, then continued slowly. "You know, it's not going to work. You have to give more notice. You have to make arrangements with a priest and have the banns posted and all that."

"We're not going to do it here. We're going down to Plattsburgh," she said. Actually, that's where she'd been that afternoon. Frédéric had driven Thomas and her down and they'd applied for the licence. It would be waiting for them Monday. Frédéric would come along to be the witness, but she wasn't going to say that to her father.

He took another sip from his whisky-soda, then sat shaking the glass slightly, watching the ice cubes knock against the sides. "And it must be next week?"

She nodded.

"You're very sure?" He looked at her steadily and she nodded again. After that, she didn't have to say anything more.

Louise couldn't imagine life without him. Thomas would be all right. All they had to do was find out where he was. Witness International had a good track record; she knew because she'd checked them out when she went looking for a project to keep Thomas occupied. Nobody was hurt on their watch.

The words ran around and around in her head while she stood in her kitchen, holding the countertop for support. Not much time had passed since the man from Witness International had said goodbye on the phone. Rosa still stood next to her, the clock had barely crept past two o'clock, the quality of light outside had not changed. But she felt as if she had gone through a profound transformation, as if the world were fundamentally different. She could not allow that, she must do what she could to keep things moving as they should. She could contact people Thomas knew — foreign affairs types, multinational wizards, even the old politicians. One of them would know something, could find out more, could arrange things. He would come back as he always had, even after those years of temptation.

"He will come back," she said aloud to Rosa. "Don't worry. He'll be perfectly all right." She was going to have to move, to act, and all the peace that had surrounded her on the island fled. Well, if that was the way it had to be, perhaps the whole purpose of her going on this retreat had been to give her the strength that she was going to need to get through this period. You never knew why things happened — the Lord truly moves in mysterious ways.

"I need some paper," she said. "Rosa, could you get me some paper? I think there's some on the table in the breakfast nook, right next to the fax machine." She gestured a little grandly, as she often did when she was overcome by emotion. "We'll make a list of who might help. We'll call everyone." She took the stack of old faxes that they used for scratch paper from Rosa and sat down at the kitchen table so she could write. "Could you get me the little telephone book too? That should be right beside the fax machine. I think that's where most of the addresses and telephone numbers are."

Then she looked up to see that Rosa was crying again. "No, Rosa, we can't have that. We can't let it get us down," she began. Then she remembered that Thomas wasn't the only one in trouble. "Oh dear," she said. "I forgot what you just told me."

Smashed glass at the Ribeira Chà. She must force herself to switch gears.

"Oh Rosa, I'm so sorry. And Manny doesn't want to call the police? How can you make an insurance claim if you don't do that?" she said, asking the question she was going to ask before the phone rang. Calling the police had to be the best thing to do. She wanted to call all of the police in the world, send out warnings, ask the highest authorities for help, anything to get closer to finding Thomas. How could Manny not want to report a blatant attack on the store?

"We don't have insurance," Rosa said. "We don't have much," she added, as if apologizing.

Louise knew that. She knew that the way she knew that the poor are always with us and that it is more blessed to give than to receive. She might not have become as involved in Rosa's life had things been otherwise. At this moment, however, she had to help. Then she could get back to her own affairs. She pushed aside the paper with the list of names she must call. "What are you going to do about the windows if you haven't got insurance?" she asked. "You'll have to get them fixed."

"That's just it," Rosa answered. "Manny was going to get his brother to bring over some plywood to cover them today, but that can't be anything more than temporary." She paused, and Louise could see how hard she was trying to keep control. What she was going to say was not going to be said easily. "I was wondering — we were wondering, that is — if you could give me an advance this month. It's going to cost a couple of hundred dollars, and we just don't have it." Her voice fell as she said the last words, but she kept her tears at bay.

Well, of course. Louise should have seen the request coming, if only in the back of her mind. Ordinarily, she never gave advances; ordinarily she tried to be very business-like. But things were hardly ordinary. "Do this," she said. "Get Manny to get a quote on how much it will cost to replace the glass — if he calls right away, he might be able to find out today. Then tell me and we'll see what we can work out."

Rosa smiled and reached her arms out toward Louise. "Oh, thank you," she said. "Thank you."

"Go now," Louise said, once again moving out of Rosa's embrace. "Go."

Rosa started down the hall toward the front door, but she stopped after only a few steps. "You'll be all right? You don't want me to do anything for you? I'm so sorry all this has happened. Poor Monsieur Brossard."

"Go," Louise said again, and forced herself to smile. "I'm fine." She held the expression while struggling to her feet, following Rosa a little way down the hall. "It'll be fine. Don't worry." When Rosa slammed the front door shut, she said to herself, "Be happy," because that was what Thomas often said.

She looked down at the list she'd been making, still in her hand. The contacts. Maybe she should telephone the contacts first because she wasn't sure what would be the best times to call the children. Richard and Anh were both working so hard they weren't likely to be back before eight or nine o'clock. There was no telling when Marielle would have a moment to telephone if Louise left a message; she was on call today and tomorrow. And Sylvain, well, where was Sylvain? Probably on the road; she'd have to contact the trucking company to find out.

Frédéric first, then. She had to talk to him about the retreat, too.

"I'm on my way," he said before she had time to explain. "Can't talk now, but I'll be there in half an hour."

A great fatigue began to settle over her, as if the effort of finding the right tone with Frédéric, with Rosa, of not being alarmist, of keeping up a good front in the face of bad things, was just too much. She could not guarantee herself that she would not break down when she called the children. She wasn't sure she could explain to whomever answered the phone in the contacts' offices what had happened. She felt herself ready to sleep. If her body could fold over, she would have put her head down on the table and slept, the way they had been forced to nap in elementary school; to return to her roots, to childhood, to the safety of old days. But she knew she should not succumb. Instead, she would reward herself, sustain herself, by checking her violets.

As soon as she shut the door to the garden room behind her, she leaned against it and felt the sweet humidity surround her.

The first African violet was a present from Thomas for her twenty-fifth birthday — *Saintpaulia ionantha*, "Englert's Diana," nestled with a tiny-leafed ivy in a brandy snifter. Very pretty. Just what she needed to see when she looked out over the frozen city from their old, two-bedroom high rise. Just what she needed when she had enough of the inside and was contemplating the energy required to pour the children into their snowsuits and go outside. Thomas had just been hired for his first real job with a future at Bell, but they were still living like poor students.

The second plant she found at the Four Brothers grocery on Saint Lawrence, on a day of thaw near the end of January. The store, even then, had an assortment of house plants, and this African violet at $1.59 had flowers just the pink of Marielle's little pouting mouth. Marielle's beautiful little mouth that old ladies stopped to coo over; the mouth that had been screeching all afternoon about a pain or a frustration that Louise could not pin down. Louise put the flower in her grocery cart, just beyond Marielle's reach. I need something for myself, she thought. After that, the flower stood on the windowsill next to the other African violet. Louise knew that she had found something — her something — to do, to be.

The house they bought was chosen with African violets in mind. When the weather improved that winter, Louise took the children to open houses on Sunday afternoons. They took the bus usually, because Thomas needed the car to get to the places where he could moonlight a little, draw-up plans for communication networks, make a little extra money.

The houses Louise chose to look at were built before the First World War for families with aspirations, as the real-estate agents said. They were red brick row houses, with maples planted in tiny front yards and room for a small garden in back. By the time Louise was making her Sunday pilgrimages, several had been divided into apartments or had become rooming houses. Others were simply stripped of their charm, as their owners ripped out the oak woodwork and chandeliers in an attempt to modernize them.

But others hadn't been touched, and with a loan from Louise's father, they could make a down payment and pay off the $30,000 mortgage with what Thomas made. The neighbourhood was not as good as the one she grew up in, but they were close enough to the best schools that the children would be able to walk.

Her violet collection grew. By Thomas's third year in parliament, it had outgrown the windowsills and she had found the money to winterize the porch and make it into a garden room. That had been a good time, and continued getting better when the Conservatives won a landslide victory in 1984, just a week before the Pope came to Canada. In many respects, it was the high point in her life, a time of sunshine, golden afternoons, cheering crowds and Thomas's picture in the newspaper, his voice on the radio, his quick, bright comments on issues before the government. She was proud of him. Of them. Only the African violets didn't do well — in the run-up to the election and the Pope's visit, she had completely forgotten them for a week at the end of August, a week of stifling heat. Several plants died from lack of water — sacrifices for victory, Thomas said when she complained.

The violets. Her passion for them grew slowly, the way her body had. She became adept at breeding them, producing marvellous plants. She knew she was not unique in the pleasure she took from them, but she kept them to herself. She shrank from meeting other people who were Saintpaulia fanciers.

Saintpaulia — the scientific name, after the man who'd sent the seeds back to Europe, Baron Walter von Saint Paul-Illaire, Commissioner for the German colony of Tanganyika.

Fanciers — what the people who were nuts about the flowers often called themselves.

Getting involved in the Saintpaulia society, entering plants in shows, would take too much energy, would infringe on her work for the Church, her children, Thomas and his projects. Besides, if she stayed clear, she wouldn't have to admit how much she dreaded entering a room filled with people she did not know.

But there it was again — the irony that Thomas had gone to Africa and she hadn't.

Thomas in Africa. Thomas in Burundi. Thomas gone missing.

Careful, she told herself. You're going to lose it. She thought of her plants, with their soft velvet leaves and their sparkling flowers. With her right forefinger, she stroked the fuzzy leaves of a plant she had picked up. Lovely plant, lovely feel.

But the panic and the anger were like warriors waiting in the bush, ready now when her defences were down, when her heart was divided with sorrow, when all her contradictions were exposed. She shut her eyes, even though she'd told Rosa a hundred times that it was one of the things not to do.

Her mind wandered, thinking of Rosa, whimpering Rosa and her problems. She put down the flowerpot and pressed her hands against her ears. She felt everything inside her coming together the way armed bands gather to attack.

"No," she said out loud. "It is not fair. It is not right. Why, when I have tried so hard to do the right thing, does all this happen to me?" She heard her voice as if coming from far away. She stood, only to catch sight of her reflection in the window of the plant room, turned into a mirror by the fading light outside. What she saw was an overweight woman with dry hair frizzing shapelessly around her head; a woman in a purple dress and tights, a smudge of potting soil across her belly; a woman who looked, to her critical eye, just two steps from ridiculousness.

"No," she said, very loudly this time. "No," she repeated again and again. It was a lament, a supplication, a reproach, a curse. But not a prayer. What she felt surpassed prayer.

For a long moment she could not tear her eyes from her reflection, but finally she leaned over, putting her hands to her face, swaying, absolutely unsure what would come next, but certain that she could not go on as she had for such a long time — trying to do the right thing, trying to make it work, to make everything work. To do what needed to be done. She deserved better. She deserved much better than this.

When Nzosaba offered to take Thomas on a tour of the city, Thomas said he'd be very pleased. What else was there to do, anyway? Sitting in the hotel and waiting was not very appealing unless you wanted to drink, and Thomas had put that behind him a long time ago. So after they left the cathedral, Nzosaba drove them up a broad boulevard, which turned to climb the range of hills that ran along the east side of the lake valley. Bigger houses here, Thomas thought. Walls around them, guards at the gates, flowering trees in bloom, a satellite dish on the roof of one. People on foot headed up the hill with loads on their heads. A Mercedes passed them on the stretch.

Then they turned off onto a relatively level area where houses made of wood and homemade bricks stood side by side and children played in unpaved lanes. "One of the new, poorer neighbourhoods," Nzosaba said. A water pipe laid and electricity brought in, a project undertaken before the last round of troubles began in 1993.

Thomas nodded sagely and asked questions about school construction and sewage, barely listening to the answers as he watched the faces of the people for signs of ... of what? Fear?

At the end of the street, Nzosaba would have continued up further into the hills, but yellow police tape marked the edge of a no-go area. "Perhaps things haven't calmed down as much as we were told. Perhaps there was an incident," he said. "Whatever the reason, we can't investigate."

So they turned down the hill, past places where women were working the soil with mattocks to prepare the next crop now that the rains had come. There seemed to be no edge to the fields, no markers, no hedges. Thomas was about to ask about property laws, when Nzosaba turned onto a lane leading toward several low buildings and a monument.

"The man who should have been king," he explained. "Gunned down at the beginning of our independence."

Prince Louis Rwagasore, Thomas remembered from the agency documents, the heir apparent who was supposed to rule the new African state. "A shame," he said.

"A tragedy," the other man said. "Had he lived, he would have rallied us all together. We would have avoided all the strife that followed."

"And who shot him?"

"You mean, who wanted him dead? A local man, a Greek, was caught right afterwards, but it's not a question of who did the act. The people who ordered his death have never been named officially."

"Belgians? Foreign investors? Another political party?" Thomas asked, realizing as he spoke that the questions were too blunt to receive decent answers. He should know better, he would have to be more diplomatic if he wanted good information.

Nzosaba shrugged. "Who knows?" Something rumbled — thunder or artillery. He turned in his seat so he could see as he backed the vehicle down the lane. "We won't stay," he said calmly. "Besides, you must be getting hungry."

In clear weather, the drive down the hill would have been spectacular, as lovely as the view across Lake Champlain from the Green Mountains to the Adirondacks. Certainly, thought Thomas, Bujumbura's setting was a lot like that of Burlington, Vermont. Both were on the edge of the flood plain formed beside a long narrow lake.

"You know," Thomas said, "this reminds me a bit of a place not far from my home."

"In Canada?" Nzosaba laughed. "I didn't think there was anything in Africa that was like Canada."

"Well actually, not Canada, across the border in the US." |77

Nzosaba looked over at Thomas. "You live that close?"

"As close as those mountains over in Zaire," Thomas answered. What he did not say is that he was suddenly reminded of the drive up the east shore of Lake Champlain the day that he entered Canada for good.

His immigration approval arrived in the middle of September — Louise's father may have been able to nudge it along a little quicker than usual — just as he received his second notice saying that he was supposed to report for induction the Tuesday after Columbus Day. It was great timing, Louise insisted. After he failed to report for the draft, he wouldn't be able to cross the border, and he had to re-enter Canada as an immigrant, not as a student. Louise thought it best to go down on the Canadian Thanksgiving weekend, which was the same as the Columbus Day holiday. A trip then would mollify Mrs. Brossard, too. She had not been pleased that they married so quickly, nor that the reception Louise's parents gave was on the Monday of Labour Day weekend. "You know I have to be at my desk when school opens the next day," she had wailed on the phone when he called to tell her the news and to invite her to the afternoon party at the Desjardins' house. She was so annoyed she never acknowledged the formal invitation Louise's parents sent by mail.

The Desjardins noted this, but seemed to think Louise's plan for a trip to Boston was a good one. "Papa will lend us his car," Louise told Thomas. "Don't worry, it will all work out beautifully."

He wasn't worrying, he assured her, but was uneasy enough about the plan to be glad when they successfully passed the first hurdle — crossing into the US — with no problem.

It was dark when they arrived in Boston, but because he wanted to show her a little of the city, Thomas drove them across the Charles and swung around by the historical heart of the city. "Look over there," he said. "See those big buildings. That's downtown. My dad lives just this side. Big luxury building, great view of the city and beyond." The old man and his second wife were in San Francisco for a tax-lawyer convention, which was all for the better. With only one full day in Boston before them, Thomas knew his mother would make a scene if they tried to see his father, but he didn't say that to Louise. Instead, he began to talk about sightseeing.

"We'll swing around so you can see some of the historic sites, even if it is dark," he said. "Faneuil Hall, where the Revolution began, and places like that."

"What Revolution?" Louise asked. She yawned and turned to look out the window. She had driven more than half the way, and then told Thomas it was his turn.

"What do you mean, 'what Revolution?'" he asked back. "The American one, of course." The traffic pattern had been changed since the last time he'd driven through here, part of the road was under construction, too. He wasn't quite sure where they were going.

"The American Revolution," she said. "Of course, I should have known. But look, when are we going to get to your mother's place? I've got to pee again."

"The Revolution against the British," he said, refusing to be side-tracked. "The one when Montreal was invaded, the one that started the whole damn thing. Don't you know that?" The question hung in the air, as if suspended from his fatigue and anxiety.

"You don't have to get mad," she said. "I didn't grow up here. Being against the English I know about, but you've got to remember that the only revolution we've had in Quebec was a quiet one."

"Sorry," he said sharply, as if he really weren't. "I forgot."

"*Je me souviens,*" Louise quoted the Quebec motto, "I remember." She sat up straighter, then wiggled her shoulders. "When are we going to get there? I'm beginning to not feel very well. You can lecture me tomorrow. Your mother can lecture me tomorrow. But tonight, it's a different story."

"We're getting there," he said. "Just hold on."

They were headed away from the historical part of town now, toward the neighbourhoods where he'd lived as a boy. Newspaper blew up in front of them from a pile of trash by the side of the road, an edge catching underneath the windshield wiper. As he flicked the wipers on, he saw that two black men dressed in jeans and leather jackets watched from beneath the streetlight. On the other corner, a woman in a miniskirt, high heels and a short fake-fur jacket leaned against a mailbox.

"We lived here when I was born," he said. "I don't remember it, of course, but every time we'd drive through the South End, my mother would talk about how hard it had been to find housing right after the war and how awful the rooming house we'd lived in was. It's a neighbourhood that hasn't got any better. Check to make sure your door is locked."

"Your mother doesn't live around here now does she?" Louise asked. She shivered a little. "This looks like a pretty dangerous place."

He knew that there'd been riots around here when Martin Luther King Jr. was killed a couple of years before. "Yeah," he said, "maybe I should have gone the other way." A sign on the corner flashed "liquor" while they waited for the next light. "Where we lived, where Mother lives now, has gone downhill too — lots of white families moving out of Jamaica Plain, lots of anxiety about school integration. The archdiocese is even talking about closing some of its schools. But her neighbourhood isn't supposed to be bad."

In fact, it looked neat and well-cared for. A street lined with three-storey buildings, an apartment on each floor, most built so that two butted up against each other, others free-standing. Little front yards, cars parked along the street, old trees. A sprinkling of leaves covered the lawns, except for one small, carefully raked patch of grass with the leaves piled into the gutter on the street.

"That's it," Thomas said. "We're on the bottom floor, and it looks like Mother has been being neat again."

Slowly, Louise stretched her legs out of the car once he'd opened the door for her. She hoisted herself up and they both stood there for a moment, breathing in the wet, spicy aroma of fall — fallen leaves, woodsmoke wafting from a fireplace in one of the houses, overlaid with the far-off, diluted smell of salt water.

Louise smiled up at Thomas and reached to touch his arm. That was when the boys appeared. They surged out of a yard, carrying nothing menacing, probably with no evil intent, just wanting to mark this street as theirs. One of them said something, and the two others laughed as they walked toward Louise and Thomas, elbowing each other, claiming the territory. Thomas ignored them and opened the back door of the car when they had passed, so he could pick up the suitcase on the back seat. "It's a different place," he said when he saw Louise looking at him questioningly, with more than a little fear in her eyes. "This country has more history than the Revolution. Not that Quebec would have been much different if you could grow cotton there."

"Cotton?" she said. "What are you talking about?"

"Slavery, but forget it. My mother is looking through the window at us, if you haven't noticed."

His mother smiled and hugged Louise, but Thomas could see right away that she did not like Louise, and Louise did not like her. He probably should have expected that. But there was more than ordinary jealousy here. As soon as he saw them together, he realized that Louise was the kind of girl his mother would have liked to have been but had been prevented from becoming. Unlike Louise, she wasn't her Daddy's darling. She was the second last girl, sent to stay with aunts because her own mother was too ill to look after her after the last baby. The aunts had done as much as they could for her — they'd sent her to a good convent school, after all — but going further was a struggle. She'd wanted to teach French, she had aspirations, yet she did something stupid, as she told Thomas and his sisters time and again — she left college so she could put their father through law school. But he left her in a swirl of accusations and sexual adventures that Thomas only appreciated once he was older. However, Thomas knew long before then that she was a very unhappy woman.

For years, she had been sustained emotionally by the pride she took in the girls — both were in nurses' training and sharing an apartment near their father — and on dreams of what Thomas might accomplish. Getting married so young was not something that she'd planned for him.

"You've made a terrible mistake," she began on Sunday afternoon when Louise was taking a nap. Thomas was standing at the sink, washing the dishes, and she was sitting at the kitchen table. They had often spent evenings during his high-school years like this, when things were not going well between her and his father. She was not going to let them slip back into that comfortable pattern. She had things to say that she wanted him to hear. She said that Louise was going to be fat before she turned thirty, that she did not seem aware of her good luck in snaring Thomas and, worst of all, that she was obviously pregnant.

"Why didn't you tell me?" she said. "Why did you let yourself get sucked into a situation like this? She's going to drag you down, now you're never going to amount to anything. You'll be stuck in a second-rate country, doing second-rate jobs with a second-rate future."

"Shhh," Thomas said. Louise was going to overhear, but it was clear his mother didn't care.

"To think I did so much for you," she continued in the loud, commanding voice she'd developed during the years when she'd done far more than her job as a school secretary required. "All those exercises to get you to walk right after you were sick. All those nights we worked on your homework together. All that work, period. You could have done anything, but no, you obviously couldn't keep your hands off her."

Her words hailed down on him, and Thomas remembered the way his father would react when she began a harangue. He would meet her accusations with shouts of his own, and the words would spiral out of control until they transformed themselves into broken dishes and slammed doors. Thomas knew he should stand up to her too, tell her his real reasons, explain about the draft notice and the immigration business. Say that it probably would be a long time before he could come back and see her. Add that he didn't want to get involved in the United States' adventure in Vietnam. What would follow, he knew, would be a huge fight, an orgy of recriminations and emotion, and he did not want shouts and tears to be his last memory of standing in his mother's kitchen. What he said was, "It's not the way it looks," before he looked around for a dish towel.

"Not the way it looks," she repeated. "Not the way it looks? Tell me what you mean, then. Tell me just what is going on." But when he refused to say anymore, she sighed as if defeated, and stood so she could reach behind him and take the dish towel from the hook, hidden by her chair back. "You'd do better to pay more attention to what you're doing. Don't be such a fool."

So he was glad to leave Boston, and glad that Louise refused to see his mother's hostility. He brooded about her bitterness, her anger, on the trip back. Louise took over the driving south of Burlington. She chattered non-stop as they drove northward along the flood plain of Lake Champlain, while he held the envelope with his immigration papers tightly in his lap. He tried to record in his head exactly how the last glow of sunset looked as it faded behind the Adirondacks on the other side of the lake. He had the feeling that he must remember these moments, that he would return to them again and again in the future for reasons he only vaguely understood.

Just before the last exit in the US, traffic slowed before it ground to a halt. "Just what we need," Louise said, looking over at him. She patted his leg.

He moved away from her touch, suddenly irritated at her attention. He wound down the window on his side and stuck his head out, even though the October air was cold. "You don't think they're backed-up all the way from the border?" he asked. Lineups going into Canada were rare, and he hadn't prepared himself for the possibility that they'd have a long wait. He wanted this to be over, he wanted his bridges burned, the milk spilt, the crying over and done with.

She saw the roadblock before he did. "There're some state troopers up ahead, that's what got us stopped," she said. "They must be looking for someone."

Thomas had seen it happen once before, the year at Brébeuf when he'd taken the bus back from Boston after the February break. The American authorities were looking for a bank robber headed toward the border, so they checked every vehicle on its way there. Two police cruisers and four officers, with weapons displayed, looked in every vehicle that passed.

They must be looking for a fugitive again, they wanted to pick up somebody on their wanted list, Thomas thought. He was no fugitive, he wasn't wanted — yet — but nevertheless, he felt ice water surge through his veins, his head and hands breaking out in a sweat. He opened his mouth to speak, but forgot what it was he intended to say. His mouth was dry, he had no breath to talk. He shifted in his seat, turning the envelope over, fighting the fear.

Then he began to open the car door. They were two cars from the roadblock. A barbed-wire fence separated the shoulder of the road from a field filled with shocks of cut cornstalks. A cloud passed over the moon.

Louise was allowing the car to roll forward when she realized what he was doing. "Stop that," she yelled at him. "Are you nuts?"

They were next. The officers were waving the car in front by.

She reached over and grabbed his jacket sleeve. "Shut that door, what the hell are you thinking?" she said to him as she turned to smile at the officer.

He had not opened the door very far, and as soon as the officer waved them on, she accelerated. The door slammed shut and she turned to him. "Are you nuts?" she repeated. "Look. I am going to drive up even with those buildings over there, and then I am going to park on the shoulder, and you are going to have to pull yourself together or this is never going to work."

He took a deep breath. He was being stupid. He knew he wasn't a fugitive, he knew they weren't looking for him. He wasn't on any wanted lists — that was the whole point of taking the trip now. He was safe so long as he acted like he should.

"Don't stop," he said. "I'm all right. I just ... I don't know."

He leaned forward and put his head in his hands, his forehead touching the dashboard. This was it, he suddenly realized. This was going to change his life more than marrying Louise had, more than deciding to become an engineer. If his mother knew what he was doing, she would call him a coward. Even his father had gone to war, she would say in that voice she used to heap scorn on the man who betrayed her. As it was, she had said Thomas was headed for a second-rate future, called him a fool.

He knew he was neither a fool nor a coward. He would not let her be right.

He sat up suddenly. "No, I'm fine," he said. "Cold feet, that's all." Then he leaned over so he could nuzzle Louise in the warm spot where her lovely neck joined her shoulder. "Got to get used to that up here, don't I?"

The rest was a piece of cake. Welcome to Canada. *Bienvenue au Québec.*

The only downer was the news that the provincial labour minister had been abducted by a band of Quebec separatists. But that didn't really affect them, insulated as they were by love and self-interest.

Nzosaba drove along in silence for a few minutes. Thomas had left Lake Champlain far behind him. This lake was much deeper and longer than the lake he and Louise had driven along as his life changed immutably. This lake was in the heart of a continent, all streams flowed into it. There was no Richelieu river, no Saint Lawrence leading to the sea and the wider world.

"And you were in the Canadian government?" Nzosaba broke the silence.

The question didn't surprise Thomas. Théophile would have explained who he was. How much to acknowledge was another question. "Yes," he said. "But out of office since the last election."

Nzosaba chuckled. "And you still live in your country! Our politicians usually can't afterward."

"Well," Thomas decided to make a joke of it, "there are some who would say that life after politics is no life at all." He wondered what Nzosaba would say if Thomas told him that he hadn't intended to become a political man, that his second big decision had started out as a joke. He could still hear Louise's laughter from the day he came home from work to announce that he was going to run for the Conservatives.

"What have they been smoking down there?" she asked when she had calmed down enough to talk. She'd been cooking dinner, and wiped her eyes on the oven mitt she'd been holding when he came in.

"Oh, they've got their reasons," he said, reaching into the liquor cabinet for the cheap bottle of Scotch. He measured a couple of fingers of whisky into two juice glasses. "Communications is a regulated industry, and Bell likes to have friends in the House of Commons." He handed her a glass and took a long drink from his. "They want to support candidates for the party that's going to win, but they also run guys for the other ones, just in case."

"But the Conservatives? The Progressive Conservatives?" she said when she'd had a drink. "Come on, they haven't elected anybody from Montreal in ages. And your friend who won the toss, he'll be an NDP candidate? Fine way to start a campaign, losing at the beginning."

But as they talked about it, she brought up things to consider, like the Red Tories who'd supported health care and Flora MacDonald who talked about Liberation Theology, even though she wasn't Catholic.

"You're right," he said halfway through his third drink. The kids were eating their meal at the kitchen table, but neither he nor Louise were hungry. The idea was crazy, but it might be possible, it might be fun. It might be what he'd been waiting for during those afternoons when he looked at his diagrams and grew annoyed with the world.

It would show his mother, too.

"They say I can have a leave of absence as soon as the election is called," he said carefully, not wanting to give away more interest than he thought he should admit to. He paused again and drained his glass. "At the very least, I could use some of the time to do a little work around here. Fix that front door for one thing, maybe paint a couple of bedrooms." Sylvain began to fuss. It was nearly his bedtime. Thomas took him out of his high chair and began to bounce him a little. "And maybe I want to do this."

Louise had begun carrying the plates to the sink. Richard and Marielle were heading down to the living room to watch television. She turned toward Thomas. "Yes," she said, stopping and looking at him directly in the eyes, "maybe you do."

"But there could be one major problem," he said.

"What's that?" she asked, reaching to take the baby. Her eyes continued steady on his, and he thought he read in them an echo of the excitement that he was feeling.

"I'm a fucking immigrant, a damn draft dodger." He said it loudly and clearly because he knew himself well enough to realize that if he didn't say it now, he might conveniently avoid thinking of it in the future.

But Louise stood up straighter and her face hardened. "So? You chose to come here. The US government gave an amnesty to guys like you two years ago. You're a man of principle. That's not a bad image to project."

He was silent — what she said was both true and not true. Sylvain started to cry. The sound of Richard and Marielle squabbling came down the hall.

"And I could help you," she said. "I know a lot of people. Let me make a few phone calls to see what's happening."

She did.

He won.

Later she said it was what they both had been waiting for, preparing for, only they didn't know it.

No matter that his election was really a fluke. He'd been only one of three Conservatives elected from Quebec that year. The riding was in central Montreal, only a district away from where he and Louise had bought their house. That wasn't what elected him however — the Liberal incumbent had quarrelled with the Liberal bigwigs, who turfed him out. The man decided to run anyway — for spite, for principle, who knew, really? — and the vote was split so that Thomas snuck down the middle.

His mother sent congratulations from Boston, but she didn't come up to see him sworn in. Five years later, the PCs swept the country. Thomas was named to the Industry and Development portfolio because the PM recognized that he'd done his job well in opposition. The fact that he was smarter than most public servants and nearly all members of parliament, that he was a quick study when it came to background documents and that he took the time to understand the details was formally recognized, but his mother didn't attend that ceremony either.

His father would have been proud, Thomas liked to think. He might even have understood what Thomas came to believe — that this second-class power had a big role to play, if only by showing the world that things didn't have to be done *à la mode américaine*. The old

man had never known Thomas's success — he dropped dead on the
tennis court, playing doubles with his second wife two weeks before
the election.

That was all over now. The government fell as governments always
fall. They'd had nine years — two mandates — which isn't bad in a
democracy, he told himself on his good days. On his bad ones, he
knew that after nearly fifteen years of public service he was spoiled for
anything else, and that was why he was here in Burundi.

The Club Nautique, where Nzosaba proposed they eat, was on the
lake. To get there, they crossed back through the commercial section
of Bujumbura, then headed south on a road that led past several tall
buildings, built in the concrete high-rise style found all over the world
— the Belgian embassy, banks, an apartment block with windows
open to the breeze. Then a bit further and a turn toward the lake, past
sheds built from unmilled wood, trees cut and split like the trunks
used to make log houses in North America.

"Are those the famous cattle?" Thomas asked as soon as he saw
what the sheds were sheltering — perhaps fifty head of black and
white cows, their coats longer and their bodies thinner than any cattle
Thomas had ever seen, even on his one mission to India. A few were
cropping the grass growing along the edge of the lake, but most of
them were clustered in front of bins, into which three short men were
forking what looked like sugar cane stalks or giant grass.

Nzosaba laughed. "I thought you'd like to see them. They were
brought in from the hills for safe keeping now that things are dangerous.
They are very important in our country."

The background sheets had said that Tutsis had been the traditional
herders and the Hutus tilled the land; that in the old days, all women
and cows belonged to the king, but the land belonged to the cows.

"Are they kept for milk or for meat?" Thomas asked. They did not
look very healthy, and he tried to remember what he'd been told about
bovine tuberculosis and undulant fever and other diseases of cattle
during those visits to dairy farms and milk processing plants at home.

Nzosaba stopped the pickup so they could get a better look. "Milk mostly. That one doesn't look too well," he added, pointing to the cow that Thomas also thought not far from death. "They need medicine, particularly now that the rains are starting. But it's so expensive even without an embargo."

Foreign exchange, countries that can't vaccinate their children, let alone their cattle, the damage that overgrazing does to hill country — Thomas could see a hundred problems, a hundred projects where outsiders might do some good. But he said nothing more; he knew he would not know where to begin.

They sat for several minutes looking at the cattle, which looked back at them. The men lifted their eyes from their tasks too, but made no other acknowledgment of their presence. Then Nzosaba drove on.

There were more cattle grazing on what looked like a soccer field as they turned down the road leading to the Club Nautique. Three cars were parked at the far end of the lot, but as Thomas and Nzosaba climbed out of the pickup and started down the walkway toward the building, the place looked empty.

"With the embargo and the troubles, I don't imagine that restaurants do much business," Thomas ventured. Three tables with sun umbrellas sat near the shore to their left, as they walked along the edge of the building. No one was sitting there.

Nzosaba nodded. "No," he said. "And I'm not sure what we'll find on the menu today."

They entered through a wide bar area, which could serve as a dance floor on happy evenings. The tables were set with orange, yellow and red cloths and napkins, but only one was taken. A light-skinned couple sat with their clasped hands on top of the table, their upper bodies leaning toward each other, as if they were waiting for a chance to kiss.

A dwarf wearing a shirt in the same bright colours as the table-cloths came forward holding menus. Nzosaba shook hands with him. "A table by the window," he said. "So we can look out at the lake."

89

The storm, whose thunder they had heard at the top of the hills, broke as soon as they sat down. Rain hammered down on the surface of the water, sending up splashes, obscuring the view as the water appeared to leap upward into the air. Two men, who had been sitting on a terrace just beyond the dining room, came hurrying in, carrying their drinks and clutching briefcases over their heads for protection. They were drenched, and a waitress, dressed in the bright, trademark colours of the place, hurried over with tablecloths to dry them off.

"Excuse me," Nzosaba said to Thomas. "I must greet these gentlemen. I'll tell the waiter to bring over a carafe of wine — you do drink wine, don't you? — and I won't be a moment."

Thomas nodded, and tried to overhear what they were talking about. He stared at the wall of water running down the picture window, trying to listen, but he could make out only the rumble of three distinct voices and, twice, "Canada." Then the dwarf came over with the carafe of wine and two wine glasses. He put one glass in front of Thomas and poured him a small amount.

"I apologize in advance," he said. "Our stock is much depleted. This is something that we would ordinarily be ashamed to serve."

Thomas sipped, smelled and nodded his head. "Not bad at all," he said. "I've drunk far worse. From France or Algeria?"

"From South Africa."

Thomas nodded again. It was all right to buy wine from South Africa; Louise had been campaigning to get the diocese to buy Mass wine from two South African wineries where the workers were being treated well. South Africa needed the foreign exchange, she kept repeating, until he wished he had never explained international monetary problems to her.

She was a smart woman. He knew he should always remember that.

The conversation between Nzosaba and the others seemed earnest and Thomas wondered if he should feel slighted. The wine began to slip into his veins, and he felt himself relaxing. Let them talk, he thought, pleased with his magnanimity. Let them talk, and I will enjoy sitting here, watching the storm.

He remembered summer storms in Montreal as intense as this one, on days just as hot and humid. During one, he and Louise had fought all afternoon. They were living with Richard and Marielle in the high rise near McGill, the same one they'd moved into after they were married. As they quarrelled, lightning flashed toward the tops of the buildings around them, illuminating the cross on the top of Mont Royal that commemorated the new colony's miraculous survival after a flood. When Thomas could no longer stand the beat of Louise's words against his back, he opened the door that led to the tiny balcony and stepped outside. The rain flooded over him then, and the electrical charge that was jumping from cloud to land and back again stirred around him.

"You idiot," Louise yelled. "You're going to be killed." A fork of lightning sliced across the sky, headed for the top of the building across the street. For an instant, all was silent, and then their ears were split by a sound louder than anything Thomas had ever known. Louise rushed forward onto the balcony, grabbed his arm, and pulled him back inside. "Come back in," she yelled, her anger at him transformed into ferocious concern. "You can't do this to me. You can't leave me a widow. You can't leave me."

He hadn't been thinking of leaving her, he was just tired of her and the kids, of a job at Bell that he already knew wasn't going to lead him where he wanted to go, wherever that was. He struggled, not knowing what it was that he did want, but before he could decide, he found her arms wrapped tight around his chest, her warm, soft body pressed against him. With no place to put his own arms, he had to wrap them around her. Holding her always sent his thoughts scattering to the wind. He could not resist her body, still could not, still found it more satisfying than that of any other woman he had known.

It was the next day that he bought her the first African violet.

He took another sip of the very good South African wine, and then another. Over the years, the plants had become almost an obsession with her, a universe she could control when she was having trouble keeping up with him.

The thunder was still roaring, but even without counting the time delay between flash and sound, Thomas could tell the storm had begun to move on. The air coming through the screened archway leading to the terrace was a bit cooler now. A mosquito, having infiltrated insidiously into the dining room, buzzed around his head.

He was in Africa because of her, because she graciously arranged for him to see sights and places that she'd been reading about for years.

The wine was nearly gone. It was good that he had been able to send a message by fax; he would thank Nzosaba again, but he also thought it would be good if he did something else for Louise, something to show her just how much he valued her opinion, her help, her love.

That is when the idea came to him — he would find the violets, he would bring her back a violet from Usumbura.

Frédéric knocked on the door to the garden room, and Louise looked up from her sorrow and her violets. "I rang the doorbell, but you didn't answer, so I let myself in," he said. "I was afraid of something like this." He still had on his winter coat — a fur-lined leather one — although he'd stopped to take off his boots.

Louise tried to wipe away her tears with her fingers, but it didn't work. "Give me a Kleenex," she said. "There on the counter, behind you."

He brought her the box, but she still leaned against the plant table, making no move toward the kitchen.

"So what's the story?" he asked. "You weren't very coherent on the phone." She could tell he didn't quite know how to play the situation. They'd known each other so long he knew most of her tricks.

She took her time wiping her face and blowing her nose, and when she was finished, she looked steadily at him. "Wait a minute, wait until I can sit down in there," she said. She slid her hands along her work counter, letting it support her tired body, until she reached the door.

Frédéric was ready to help her, but she pushed aside his arm, and willed herself to cross the kitchen to her place at the table.

"I don't know much," she began. He listened carefully, bouncing slightly up and down on the balls of his feet, as if wondering how he should go into action. "I must make some more phone calls," she said as she finished. "The kids to begin with, I guess, and then anyone who might have some information. I made a list."

94 | Frédéric nodded, but didn't say anything. He did not move to take off his coat, to sit down, to comment on what she'd said.

"What do you think?" she asked. "Can you see anything better to do?" She watched the way his eyes seemed to look inward, his long grey hair fluffed around his head like a halo, and she wondered, once again, where his heart lay.

He passed his right hand over his face and rubbed his eyes. "Poor Thomas," he said. "Poor you." Then, standing up straighter, as if shaking off bad thoughts — "Do you have any idea what the motive might be? I mean, is this a kidnapping for a ransom? Or is he a bargaining chip?"

"Don't say that," she said. "Let's not talk about that. Let's hope the next thing we hear is that he's safe."

"But there is that possibility," he began.

"Yes," she cut in. "There is. But I don't know that I can face it now."

"Kidnapping would be better than a massacre," he said simply. When she didn't comment on that, he asked, "Do you want me to make the calls? You think you can handle talking to the kids?"

"They won't be there probably, not at this hour, they'll be out doing whatever. So I'll call them. If they get a message from you, they'll worry too much ..."

He laughed. "They have reason to worry," he said. "You mean you don't want them to panic."

"Not my kids," she turned. "They're too level-headed."

"Like their mother. But I'll call whoever else you want — journalists, foreign affairs?"

Before she could answer, the phone rang. She smiled quickly at him and eagerly reached for the receiver. "Maybe good news already," she said.

But the voice wasn't that of the Witness International man. "Madame Brossard," Rosa said. "I'm sorry to bother you again."

Louise shut her eyes and swallowed. Once again, she had forgotten about the smashed glass at the Ribeira Chà. She forced herself to sound calm. "Yes, of course," she said. "Your husband was able to get an estimate for the work already?" she asked. She looked at the clock, maybe an hour had passed since Rosa left; time enough for Manny to contact a glass company if he'd started looking right away.

There was a silence on the end of the line, and Louise wondered if Rosa would give her an argument about how she shouldn't help them. "Tell me how much it is," she said. "Tell me straight, and let's not play around. I prize your help, and you have never asked for an advance before, so I'd be glad ..."

Rosa gave an embarrassed laugh. "Well," she said, "it's like this. Manny thinks he may have a way out. We might be able to get by." She paused, swallowed. Louise was sure that Manny told her to say that. She was equally sure from the tone of Rosa's voice that Rosa did not agree. "But if you really want to help, it would be wonderful. You have no idea ..."

Louise didn't want her to go on. "Tell me how much it will be. Do you have a formal estimate? Do you need to pay in advance?" Given all of Ribeira Chà's problems, she was sure that nobody would give them any credit.

Rosa said nothing for a moment, and Louise thought she heard Manny prompt her from the background, urging Rosa to say that she was sorry to call under the circumstances. Louise did not want to hear condolences. "How much?"

"It's rather high, three-hundred and fifty dollars," Rosa said, and fell silent.

"Three-hundred and fifty," she repeated, glancing over at Frédéric. "Look," she said after a moment, "I'll get back to you later. There are some things we've got to do now. But don't worry, go ahead and make arrangements to replace the glass. I'll be in touch soon." She hung up before anything more could be said.

"You don't have three-hundred and fifty dollars on you by chance, do you?" she asked Frédéric before he could ask her what all that was about. "My cleaning woman and her husband have a crisis, and I don't have anything like that in the house. Whereas, you" — and she smiled briefly — "you seem to have a lot of money to throw around lately."

"They didn't say anything about me on the island, did they?" He looked worried. "It was supposed to be anonymous."

"It was. Only a select few have any idea. Almost everyone there thought it was a simple miracle." She picked up the phone again and dialed Richard's number in Cambridge. "The kids first."

As she expected, they weren't home. She left a message on the answering machine. With Marielle, the pediatric service she was working at for the academic session took a message, and for Sylvain, it was the dispatcher at the trucking company. When she finished, she called Witness International again, just to see if there was any news. There wasn't. After that, she looked up the number of the deputy minister Thomas most trusted at Foreign Affairs and the number of the former prime minister's assistant, who sat on the boards of two or three companies that did business in Africa.

"Not Brian himself?" Frédéric asked, looking at the numbers. "I thought he was always looking out for his people."

Louise laughed. "It's been a long time since Thomas was one of his people. I get so angry when I think of all the things he went through to be a good team player. There was that time when ..." She stopped herself because she didn't want to think about it.

The worst had been the summer of 1990. There was that fight about a constitutional accord, Indians at Oka blocking roads and a by-election that turned out to be the first test for a breakaway group of Quebec nationalists, the Bloc Québécois. In retrospect, it was the beginning of the end.

Thomas wanted Louise to go to the opening of an art exhibition at the Montreal Museum of Fine Arts. She was annoyed he even suggested it. "No," she said the Saturday morning he brought it up. She was sitting in the armchair by the window in their bedroom, wearing just a summer nightgown, but already she could feel the sweat trickling down between her breasts. "I don't do that kind of thing. You know that." Just the thought of entering the building and going up the great staircase to the exhibit made her ill. She would be on display, she would be at risk.

There was more behind her reluctance, though. There were politics involved — international, world-shaking politics, of which Thomas should be made aware. Probably he did know — as Minister of Industry he was heading the project for the aerospace plant that Oerlikon was building in the eastern townships — but she had to make sure. Because she knew he listened best when she sounded sweet, she willed her voice to be charming when she started to explain. "I'd do most anything for you, my love," she began.

He was lying on their bed with the covers thrown back. Aside from the whir of the fan in the corner and the rustle of the drawn curtains, the house was quiet. Richard had a summer job planting trees up north, Marielle was a junior counsellor at a camp in the townships and Sylvain was still asleep in the basement.

As she spoke, she saw Thomas's eyes flick toward her and a little smile turn up the corners of his mouth. He had a nice smile, she'd always liked it, it had served him well in all those political meetings. She couldn't let its charm influence her now. There were big issues at stake. "You know, *mon coeur*, the idea of spending a hot summer evening looking at pictures is not very inviting."

He didn't say anything — he knew very well how she hated both heat and public appearances — but his smile faded. "Besides," she went on, "I got a fax this week from the Catholic Peace Network." She paused to see if he would react, but he was examining his thumb as if that were more important than what she was saying. He could guess where she was heading, even if he didn't know exactly what she was worried about.

"Do you know how that Oerlikon guy, Burley, or whatever his name is, made his money?" she asked, but she didn't wait for him to answer. "Selling arms to the Nazis, that's how." She let that sink in before she continued. "And do you know where the paintings came from? A lot of them were stolen from Jews. The exhibit is mostly just a display of the spoils of war."

He didn't react immediately, but then, he almost always gave himself a second to run through the possibilities — it was a trick he learned on the floor of the House of Commons. He continued to look at his hands, gnawing for a second on his thumbnail while he prepared his line of attack. "Spoils of war?" he said, the words coming slowly. "You don't know what you're talking about. Oerlikon's a Swiss company, Bührle died in Switzerland. Switzerland is neutral, always has been. You should know that."

"Yes," she said. "I do, but being neutral cuts two ways. The Peace Network has proof that Oerlikon shipped arms to Germany until late 1944. And now it's supplying arms to South Africa, Iran, Argentina ..."

"Spoils of war?" he said again, interrupting her. He pushed himself up on his elbow so he could look at her more easily. "That's a crazy thing to say. Your Peace Network is around the bend on this one."

"Nevertheless," she began, but he didn't let her go any further.

"This exhibit is full of universally accepted masterpieces," he said. "We're talking about an art show put on by a family foundation that co-operates with non-profits all over the world." He gave a little laugh and waved his free hand in the air, as if pushing aside her words. His voice shifted to attack mode, the one he used when answering during question period, the one he'd honed in hours of raucous parliamentary debate. "Your peace people are nuts," he said. "Jewish paintings? Spoils of war? Did you know that the Israel-Quebec Friendship

Committee is putting on a fundraiser at the museum the day after the show opens? With the blessing of the Bührle foundation, for God's sake. Do you think they'd sign on if Bührle was a Nazi war criminal?"

She ignored the question. "The show is not the only thing, there's a lot more going on here," she said. "You haven't forgotten that business about the land Oerlikon bought down on the Richelieu to build its plant? One of your friends in caucus had to resign over that, didn't he? His assistant's got criminal charges pending still." She was trying to keep her voice light and pleasant, but knew that an edge was creeping in because what she was saying was so damning. Influence peddling, kickbacks — there always were rumours about them in politics, but the allegations had got to the courts this time. The PM was taking the high road, but he always would.

Thomas laid back. He shifted the pillow under his head — it was his turn to ignore what she was saying.

"You probably shouldn't even go to the opening of the exhibit, you should be noticeably absent and make a statement about good government," she said. "Like Caesar's wife, you know, not only virtuous but having the appearance of virtue."

He turned his bare back toward her and kicked his legs against the sheets. "Virtue," he said. "Louise, you don't know what you're talking about."

"But I do," she said. "And besides, even if you have to go because you're the Minister of Industry and somebody thinks the government should acknowledge all the investment that Oerlikon is making, there's no reason why his wife has to be there."

Thomas did not reply immediately. When he did, he said, "We need to get an air conditioner. That's what I like about my place in Ottawa, it's got central air conditioning."

"And when you spend time there during the summer, you always come back with a cold," she said. "No, you're changing the subject." She came over to sit on the edge of the bed and took his hand, which had been lying, unclenched, on the sheet. It was too hot, she didn't want to make love again, but she knew that the best way to get his attention was to touch him. "You've got enough to do right now — the by-election, the trade negotiations. Is going to a reception at a museum going to help any of that?"

"Yes," he said, turning so he could look at her squarely. "Yes," he said again for emphasis. "I do not ask you to do things like this very often, but occasionally you have to be there. This is one of them." His eyes drilled into her, as if they could force her to do what he wanted. "The boss wants you there, too. It's important. There are things going on, there are pressures," he began, but didn't go on.

She didn't want to think what the pressures might be. She dropped his hand.

"No, listen," he said, but hesitated for a second before continuing, as if weighing which tactic to use. Then, obviously, he opted to change his form of attack. He rolled onto his elbow, so his face was right next to the roundness of her hip, which he began to run his fingers over lightly. "The exhibit's called 'The Passionate Eye,'" he said softly. He rubbed his cheek against her body and sighed deeply, almost theatrically. "Don't you think that sounds interesting?"

She sat up straighter, pulling herself slightly away from him. "It's too hot," she said.

For several minutes, they stayed like that. The clock ticked, and Thomas's fingers traced patterns on her hip, wider and wider each time, ruffling her nightgown, pushing it up and moving closer to her bare skin. As she sat there, still on her guard, she ran through her options — she could not avoid the stories that circulated about him and women in Ottawa, and usually she met any advance from him with warmth because, over the years, she had decided that sex was the glue which held couples together.

"All right," she said finally. "I'll go. But I won't stay long."

He was smiling, sitting up; he was taking her by the shoulders and pushing her down. "Good," he said before he covered her mouth with his. "Good," he whispered in her ear when he was done, and she

THE VIOLETS OF USAMBARA

was ready to smile up at him, despite the sweat that covered her.

That was Saturday. A Saturday when he left the house shortly before noon to campaign with the by-election candidate and the young woman who ran his riding office. Louise kissed him at the front door, watching while the girl held the back door of the car open for him before climbing in front with the driver. A nice looking girl involved with a young lawyer working for the Crown Attorney's office in Montreal. Not a woman to worry about, Louise told herself. Nevertheless, she was glad she had agreed to what he wanted in the end.

She decided that she would buy a new dress. An expensive dress; let Thomas pay for the privilege of her company. No matter that she had to get a size bigger than she had the last time — the dress was fine cotton in just the right shade of mauve, with a sliver-thin line of darker purple at three-inch intervals. She thought she looked terrific in it, and the light fabric would be cool in the heat outside, while the long, loose sleeves would provide protection from the air conditioning inside.

She said she'd meet Thomas at the museum at about five thirty, but had forgotten about rush hour on Sherbrooke Street. Traffic had to squeeze by heavy equipment being used to build the new museum across the street, and after ten minutes of gridlock, she had the driver let her off a block away. That meant she was covered in sweat, and her high-heeled shoes — ones she'd found in the back of her closet that were the same shade as the stripe in the dress — had begun to rub on her little toes by the time she arrived at the broad stairs that led up to the museum entrance.

This is the last time, she told herself as she stood at a table where two young women were checking names off the invitation list. I won't let him talk me into doing anything else like this, she thought. There is no reason for me to, and my being here will make no difference in the world.

She saw a few familiar faces in the crowd mounting the curving staircase toward the second level where the exhibition was installed.

She put a careful, pleasant expression on her face and slowly climbed up, one slow step after another. Mila Mulroney was there, she held out her hand to Louise, kissed her on both cheeks, then swept over to the next person. The perfect political wife, Louise thought, not meaning it as a compliment. Then out of sheer exasperation with doing everything the usual way, she turned to her left instead of the right to enter the exhibit.

She was greeted by two big paintings of the canals of Venice. They must have been five feet wide and four feet tall, as big a view as you might see from a particularly well-placed hotel balcony. Like a photograph, she thought, only she knew she was seeing more than she ever had looking at a photo mural. She stared and held her breath, as if she might fall forward into the picture were she not careful. She felt as if she had suddenly been transported into another time, another world.

An excerpt from the exhibit's catalogue, posted near the entrance to the room, suggested that escaping the ordinary world was, indeed, one of the reasons Bührle collected these paintings. It said he would go late at night into the annex, where he stored the art he had collected over thirty-five years, and walk among them as if this were a "refuge, a place where the 'spinning globe' stood still and ... the important thing was not mere display or discussion, but reflection."

Imagine being able to stroll among paintings like this on sleepless nights. Imagine owning *Olive Orchard* by Van Gogh, where the leaves and the bits of sky and the ground itself seem to vibrate with energy. Imagine stopping to rest in front of the field of red poppies Monet painted in 1879.

Imagine having the money to buy all this.

And then, inevitably — imagine what it took to make the money.

That was it, of course. Even though it was not mentioned anywhere in the catalogue or on the explanatory signs, there was no getting around the fact that Oerlikon's millions — maybe even billions — came from making arms, and Bührle's fortune came from Oerlikon.

Damn, Louise said to herself. Here we are, nearly a year after the fall of the Berlin Wall, when we thought the peace we'd prayed for was upon us, and I'm overwhelmed by beauty bought with blood money.

A great wave of guilt swept over her. She was mortified that she admired these things, that for even a minute she envied the man who had brought them together with the spoils of war. She wanted to erase what she'd been feeling. She wanted to go home and strip off this beautiful dress and tear it up for cleaning rags. A penance for being involved in this world that was so morally suspect.

She looked around for Thomas, more annoyed than ever that he'd put her in such a situation. A waiter came by with a tray of sparkling wine. She took a glass and began to walk through the exhibit rooms. The halls were filling up, the air conditioning was having trouble keeping a comfortable temperature, the sound of many voices filled the space.

She might have missed the painting had she not been jostled by a knot of people moving backward to make room for another waiter. When she stopped, her eye caught the title before it lighted on the painting — *Kandinsky with African Violet and Parrot*.

The picture was a vertical rectangle with the head and shoulders of a man taking up much of its upper-left portion. A thin man, with a neatly trimmed beard and mustache, wearing wire-rimmed spectacles and a sky blue jacket and scarf. He was looking down and to his right, out of the picture. His face was peaceful and gauntly handsome, making Louise think of Christ in any number of Last Suppers. To his left, a wall was covered in hay yellow wallpaper. Behind him, the sprigged pattern was lost against a swath of grey-green that reminded Louise of the shade under spruce trees in high summer.

In front of him, on a table covered with the same grey-green, sat a blue pot filled with dark red flowers that she would never have recognized as African violets without the title as a clue. By Gabriele Münter, the card said, painted in 1910. Baron Walter, the German colonial official who'd found the plant in the East Usambara mountains, was supposed to have sent his seeds back to his father in Berlin a good fifteen years before 1910. All the sources said that within a very short time the flower was grown everywhere, and there it was, at the centre of one woman's portrait of a man she clearly loved.

The world is complicated, Louise thought. I can't help it, I like this picture anyway. I would love to own it, I would love to be able to see its blues — the colour of masculinity, the explanatory placard said — and its yellows — the colour of femininity — and to wonder who had bred the lovely flowers and placed them there.

Thomas found her still standing in front of the painting ten minutes later. He came up behind her and put his arm around her shoulder. "So, you discovered it," he whispered in her ear.

She turned to look at him, her smile broad, her heart leaping out toward him. "You saw it before?" she asked.

"The Oerlikon people showed me the catalogue a week ago, and when I leafed through it, it opened to the picture. Pure chance." He peered at the painting, pushing his head forward, but still hugging her. "Doesn't look much like an African violet, though."

"And that's why you insisted I come?" she said. She felt tears start to sting her eyes, completely unbidden.

He smiled. "Partly," he said. "Never doubt that I know what my Loulou likes." He kissed her a little theatrically on her forehead and held her hand for a moment while his blue eyes — which she had always loved — held her gaze. "Come over here with me. I want you to meet some people."

She should have guessed what would come next. The signs were all pointing that way, the picture with the African violet was just a happy coincidence for him. He introduced her to Emil Bührle's daughter and to the vice-president of Oerlikon Canada as "my wife, the force behind Catholic charities in Montreal." Like the benefit for the Jewish cause, her presence conveyed the message that all was forgiven. Oerlikon was a good corporate citizen, Thomas Brossard was a team player, nobody in government or industry should worry where his sentiments lay.

Then it was over, and he was leading her to a place where she could sit down. "Thank you," he said. "I know how difficult that was, but there's a little tug of war going on. You understand, don't you?"

She didn't, quite, but she nodded because her mind and body were in such turmoil that she couldn't do otherwise.

"I have to go back to Ottawa tonight," he said. "I'll call, but I probably won't be home before the weekend." | 105

She nodded again. Afterwards, as she brooded back at home over a couple of whisky-sodas, she decided his absence was a good thing. He had betrayed her, he had used her to give legitimacy to whatever struggle was being played out in the government. It was just as well he wasn't around for a while — she knew that she was not going to be able to control what she might say to him. She needed time to reflect on how their missions fit together. So she let him go in peace, even if there was very little of it in the world.

She later heard that Bührle's son was decorated by South Africa's apartheid government for selling it arms clandestinely during those years of international embargo.

Arms to Africa — all those conflicts, all those guns. In the next few years, as she learned more, she wasn't even surprised that the AK–47 was displayed on the flag of Mozambique, along with a mattock and a book. She had read in a report on child soldiers that the Kalashnikov was designed during World War Two by a patriotic Russian to use against the Germans. It was perfected too late for that, but just in time for colonial wars. Millions had been made from pirating Kalashnikov's plans, maybe as much as Oerlikon made on its big guns. Follow the money and it will tell you a tale, Louise thought.

Frédéric was explaining on the telephone — "We thought you should know. No, there isn't much that can be done now, but if we don't hear more by tomorrow morning, we might like you to see what you can find out." His voice was smooth, he acted with authority. It was his commission manner, the one he used when he dealt with his major clients.

He put the phone down and looked over at her. "Have you had anything to eat yet, my dear? And what do you have to drink?" he asked.

The clock read after three now, and she realized that she hadn't had anything since the skimpy breakfast at the retreat. The eggs and toast that Rosa was going to fix had been forgotten in the commotion. "Look in that cupboard there. I know there are some crackers and smoked oysters." She needed to eat, she had to be careful, she couldn't let herself lose control.

He pulled three flat cans and a box of Wheat Thins out and put them on the counter. "Hors d'oeuvres," he said, pulling the tab back on a can. He put an oyster on a cracker and handed it to her. "There. That's a beginning."

The salty, smoky taste rolled around on her tongue, stirring-up appetites. She licked her fingers and stood up carefully, her legs rebelling; her body did not like this tension. "That tastes good," she said, going over to the counter and starting to put oysters on more crackers.

"Don't eat too many. I'll make something more substantial and we'll have an early supper," he said. "In a time like this, you need my famous spaghetti sauce."

Louise smiled. She knew men who could cook, even men who cooked for a living, but every single one of them had a recipe they fell back on in times of stress. "All right," she said. "You get it started, and then we must see about getting some money for Rosa."

He nodded as he began opening cupboards, looking for saucepans, canned tomatoes or God only knows what. "There is a money machine on Park Avenue," he said. "We'll go over there and you can make a withdrawal, then we'll take it by Rosa's before we go to church. You're going to want to say a prayer and light a candle, right?"

106|

"You'll come with me? You want to go to church?" She found her smile broadening. She hoped he could find comfort — she needed his company.

There had been a time when Frédéric was the one whose spiritual life had been the stronger. The summer after he and Louise played Atala and Chactas on the Île d'Orléans, he didn't come to visit. He did a retreat instead, took courses at the seminary, was busy elsewhere, his mother said. Maybe he would visit at the end of the summer, after he'd seen his father in Vancouver. His parents were divorced, for reasons that no adult ever spoke about in front of the children.

Louise missed him the first week she was on the island, but by the second, she'd discovered that one of the houses down the road toward the village — a new house, built fifteen years ago by the son of one of the old families — had been sold to people from Quebec City. Not only did they have a daughter the same age as Louise, they were also building a swimming pool.

What followed was a dreamy summer of watching the workmen — two were young and already golden brown from working outside — and lying around the pool, turning brown themselves. Frédéric wrote only once, a short note on lined paper torn from an exercise book. All was well; he was busy and growing in grace.

Louise did not share the note with her new friend because she was afraid the other girl would laugh. Louise thought it was a little funny herself, but she also thought she knew what Frédéric was trying to do. She admired him for it. She knew all about vocations; the nuns talked about them often. For six months when she was thirteen, she had checked her own faith every hour or so, to see if it had suddenly blossomed into a vocation, the way snowdrops and trilliums appear at the end of winter through melting snow and last year's leaves.

By the time she was finishing high school, she knew she didn't have one. Questions of faith and good works still concerned her, as they would all her life, but she could not imagine living without the thrills that she classed under one big heading — Boys. She did not understand how nuns could have chosen a life removed from all that excitement.

Frédéric himself did not last at the seminary. Within a year he was out, studying architecture, looking good when she saw him at Christmas. Was that when he decided he was gay? She never knew, she never asked. She didn't know for sure about him, until the night he came to them for help after Richard was born. She and Thomas were living in the high rise, and she was pregnant with Marielle.

Thomas answered the door, since she was struggling to get the baby ready for bed. She expected to hear the voice of the old lady who lived in the end apartment. Visitors from outside were supposed to be buzzed in from the lobby, and the intercom had been silent.

"What the hell?" she heard Thomas say, and she peeked around the door jamb from the bedroom to see what was happening. Then she heard Frédéric say, "Let me in, let me in," before he began to cry. She hurried out, holding the baby close to her, as if she knew in advance that she would find a scene Richard should not see.

"No," Thomas said to her. "Back in there. Let me handle this." He tried to spin her around, to send her back to the safety of the other room, but before he did, she saw Frédéric's face covered in blood. The smell of vomit and sweat hit her from across the room.

"Thank you, thank you," Frédéric was whispering. "I waited outside until someone didn't shut the front door completely. I didn't know where else to go." He began to step toward Thomas, but then slowly crumpled to the floor.

Thomas did the cleaning up. "Rock the kid until he falls asleep," he ordered. "Then just stay in there. I'll tell you when to come out."

As he worked on the cut above Frédéric's eye, he heard the complete story, more or less. How Frédéric had met the man in a bar, the way he had met other men. What had begun as a dangerous game had become much rougher than usual. The explosion of violence was too much, the fists, the boots, the flurry of pain, release and redemption were followed this time by a knife.

Over the years, Louise came to know several gay men, among them an organist who played occasionally at Sainte-Anne-d'Outremont, Thomas's administrative assistant in Ottawa and the couple who bought and renovated the house next door. None of them, it seemed to Louise, raged against their nature the way Frédéric did. Part of this, she realized, came from the fact that the others were all younger, all men who discovered what they liked at a time when loving other men was more accepted.

She suspected that there was something else that maintained the circle in which Frédéric came to live — abstinence, surrender, violence, repentance. He might have been seduced, abused, physically and psychologically damaged by a priest or teaching brother, but Louise never asked. In the end, she decided it did not matter if he had. His agony came from the conflict between his body and his faith. He loved men, which was forbidden. He could not lose himself in the flesh of a woman, of a wife. Each time his body ached for another, he was in a state of apprehended sin. He should repent, he must confess, he would require penance. From there, it was only a small step to mixing the passion with the punishment, for finding true release only when the flesh was mortified.

After that first time, when he spent the night on their sofa and Thomas protected her from the worst, he would often arrive early on Sunday mornings to go with her to Mass. Usually, he did not confess or take the sacrament, but would sit beside her and pray. Often, he would be wearing clothes that he must have been wearing the night before. Once, she wanted him to borrow a clean shirt from Thomas because his own was so dirty, but she did that only once. He looked at her with an intensity that she'd never seen before, turned around, and walked out of the house, not bothering to shut the front door.

After that, she took him as he was, in whatever condition he was. He continued to work as an architect, developing a reputation for buildings that combined glass and wood in what he called the ice and forest dyad. He did the corporate headquarters on the outskirts of Ottawa for a pharmaceutical company and designed the principal residence for a world-famous singer from Quebec. He supervised dozens of smaller projects — caisses populaires, new wings to CEGEPs, factories converted to condominiums. He earned a lot of money.

Much of which he gave away.

"Are you going to explain why you bailed out the retreat?" Louise asked, watching him get out the chopping board, the onions, a knife and begin the preparations for his spaghetti sauce.

"You're changing the subject," he said. "But if you must know, my spiritual advisor suggested it." He looked over at her, holding a chunk of onion on the tip of the knife.

"And who is that?" she asked.

"If you don't know, then I'm not telling you," he said. "We need some wine. You can't make spaghetti sauce without wine. And where is your Italian sausage? I think we'll need that too."

"There is no sausage, there is no unfrozen meat. This is not a grocery store," she said. "Who told you to make the donation?"

Frédéric said nothing as he finished chopping the onion and putting it into the frying pan. "You did, my dear, you did," he said finally.

Louise shut her eyes. It was the kind of answer she both hoped for and feared. "Really?" she asked. "I helped show the way?" She'd tried to convince him to come with her to the retreat for meditation and prayer several times, but he never had, he hadn't visited the Île d'Orléans since his mother died. Over the years, Louise made sure he knew about what was going on at the Fellowship of Saint Laurent. She shared with him her excitement when it acquired a Victorian country house on the island ten years before. In the summers before Atala and Chactas, she and Frédéric had often ridden by it on their bicycles. Twice they had stealthily explored its gardens when the widow of the railroad baron who'd built it was living there. Louise told him how the childless old woman bequeathed the house and five acres to the Fellowship, and she kept him informed when the old man's nephews contested the will. The Fellowship won, but now the debt incurred fighting the legal challenges was breaking its back.

"You know what fine work goes on there?" she said. "The general who tried to save the Rwandans came to speak last weekend. You can imagine what effect he can have, the inspiration, the call for action."

"I know," Frédéric said. "I know all that. Besides, it seemed to me that a small gift would be an appropriate way to celebrate." He took care not to look at her as he said this.

"Celebrate what?" she asked. She was instantly on guard; his face was set and serious. He liked celebrations, but usually when he talked about them his face was lit up with mischief. This was something different.

"We're coming clean," he said, still stirring, still not looking at her. He paused. She thought for a second his hesitation was for effect — he was a good storyteller, he knew all the rhetorical tricks — but the fact that no smile appeared to be hiding in his eyes emphasized the importance of what he was saying. "My friend's moved in, he's told his wife, he's going to tell his boss." He stopped and turned so he could finally look at Louise. "I've never been so happy."

He did look happy at that moment — a smile spread across his face the way sunshine washes the countryside as the clouds roll away. It was a smile of deep pleasure, one that even smoothed away the lines around his eyes. He looked adolescent, a romantic, as if he were completely captured by whatever this was. But life was more than that, Louise knew.

"Your friend," she said. "A man?"

"Of course," he said. "You know me well enough to know that."

"How old is this guy?" she asked after a moment.

"Late thirties. Someone who's lived a little, someone not too young for me."

"Married, you said? Any kids?"

Frédéric didn't say anything for a moment, holding back before he looked straight at her. "Five. But I'm not going to take him away from them."

Five kids. Louise heard herself breathe in sharply. She turned away from him, looking around for a task to busy herself with. She didn't want to let him know what she thought of that, of five kids and a man who had decided he was homosexual, until she had a chance to consider the implications.

"You don't approve, do you?" he said, watching her back.

She didn't answer. Of course she did not approve. She loved Frédéric

like a brother — more than a brother — and she needed him now.

"Do you think it's better to live a lie, to have to sneak around, and all that soap opera crap?" he asked. "I'm tired of it. I'm so tired." He put down the spatula and went over to stand beside her, but he didn't touch her. "It has not been easy. I did not choose the way I am, and I have been hurt so many, many times." There was nearly a sob in his voice. She was sure it was sincere, but the idea chilled her nonetheless. "But I am growing older," he said, "the rough stuff has been too much for me for a long time. I need to take this chance for some happiness before it gets away." He stopped, as if waiting for her to speak, but when she didn't, he went on. "Do you understand? You and Thomas have had years and years of something. Why can't I have some too?"

"But it's a sin," she began before she had finished considering her words.

"A sin? So is birth control, but, my dear, pious darling, you only have three children."

"It's not the same."

"It is the same. And now I want to thank God for giving me some-one to love who loves me back." His words were coming so fast now that he spit a little and didn't notice. "Oh, Louise, if he hadn't been such a nice guy, such a very nice guy, someone who didn't want to hurt anybody by being true to himself, he would have left his horrible wife a long time ago. He wouldn't have let her manipulate him, he never would have forced himself, there wouldn't be five children. He wouldn't be vulnerable, he wouldn't be trying to climb out from under a ton of abuse and worry and blackmail and ..."

The word blackmail registered deep in her consciousness, but the front of Louise's mind was taken up with sudden understanding of why Frédéric had been so circumspect about giving the money.

"So that's why you wanted to be anonymous," she said. "You've been bargaining with God. You said to yourself, and to Him, that you would rescue the retreat if God would give you what you wanted. But you knew the gift would be turned down if Brother Jean-Marie knew what your motivation was."

Then more suspicions hit her. "And where'd the money come from? Is there something fishy going on there? Tell me Frédéric, I want to know."

"No, no, the money's honest money, as honest as money ever is," Frédéric scrambled to say. "The stock market's taken off, I just followed tips my *copain* gave me. He takes care of your portfolio, too. You should be doing as well."

His friend was also their friend, the one who'd managed their affairs when Thomas put everything in the blind trust, who'd given her good advice since then. "So this has been going on for a long time, this romance?" Louise asked.

"In a manner of speaking, yes. Our paths first crossed years ago." He stopped and swallowed, as if he were considering how much to tell her. He put his arm around her shoulder and squeezed her to him. "Oh Louise, he's never been ready to admit it publicly until now. Don't you see? This is what I've been hoping for years." She looked up at him to see how his eyes sparkled, how much he looked like someone who'd won a lottery. "I'm so thankful," he said. "And as for giving the money away, isn't that what religion is built on? What finances the Church? What pays the priests and the missionaries? Guilt and bargaining and thanks when things go well."

Louise slipped away from him, stepping just far enough back to underline her disapproval. "It shouldn't be like that. You should give out of the fullness of your heart. You can't negotiate with God."

"My dear Louise, what you're saying is bullshit," he said, turning again to look at her. "The whole world tries to negotiate with God."

"No, it's not like that ..." But he wouldn't let her go on.

"Be honest with yourself," he said. "You know why you get yourself involved in Africa, why you sent Thomas off to do good there. If Africa didn't exist, you'd have to invent it because you need some faraway place where you can earn your salvation. Besides, you know how it works, you know how much it all costs, you know that guilt is what keeps it all going ..."

But he was wrong, it was not guilt that drove her. "No," she started to say.

A sudden whoosh came from the forgotten frying pan, as the hot olive oil burst into flame. Frédéric whirled around at the sound, and stared, immobile, uncertain what to do. Louise snatched up the cutting board from the counter where Frédéric had been working and moving faster than she imagined she could, brought it down on the blazing frying pan, smothering the flames.

"Don't do that," he said, "it'll catch fire too." But he didn't move to do anything else.

She turned off the gas under the pan and counted to thirty, not looking at him. When she lifted the cutting board, smoke poured out, but there were no flames. "Open the back door," she said. "Get out of my way." She grabbed a pot holder, and carrying the pan with both hands, she started for the door at the far end of the kitchen. "Open the door," she repeated, as Frédéric hesitated. With the cold air flowing in, she quickly went out on the back steps and threw the pan into the snow.

"You have a lot to learn about domesticity," she said when she came back inside.

"I'm sorry," he began. "I'm not used to cooking."

She looked at him, wondering if she should say more. But she was tired; her heart was pumping so hard she felt it might break. She did not need to stress her body like that, particularly when her spirit was so troubled. She sat down at the kitchen table. "Don't apologize," she said. "We won't speak of it again. We'll order in something later. Now, however, I must go to the money machine, I must pay Rosa and then I must go to church." She reached for the telephone to call a cab.

"May I still come with you?" Frédéric asked.

She didn't answer, but gave the address to the taxi dispatcher. She turned to the plate of oysters and crackers that she'd left on the table and began to stuff her mouth. When she'd finished, she leaned over to look for her boots, which were still under the kitchen table.

"May I?" he asked again.

Again, she said nothing, and began to struggle to pull the boots on. When he knelt before her, she allowed him to help her slide the zipper up over her calf. She also allowed herself one small, quick memory of the island and a summer day — the story of Atala and Chactas and the way he warmed her feet with his hands.

The sun was setting by the time they reached the Ribeira Chà. The fresh snow reflected back the light from the sky, burnt pale blue and green by the round, blood red setting sun. Clearly, it was the end of the work day. Park Avenue was filled with a steady stream of buses and cars, while the side streets were clogged by vehicles trying to get around the remaining snow piles. Their taxi took nearly ten minutes to navigate the three blocks from the bank machine and liquor store — "I saw you have no gin," Frédéric said, "we have to stop and get some" — to Saint-Viateur, where Manny and Rosa's store was located.

From a block away, Louise could see Ribeira Chà's windows covered with plywood. As they inched their way toward the store, she saw Manny come out with a small man wearing what looked like a suit and tie under a heavy, but unbuttoned, Kanuk winter coat. They were talking intently, and as the taxi pulled up, Louise saw that Manny's eyebrows were drawn together in concern.

She let Frédéric pay the driver as she struggled her way out of the cab. Then she stood for a moment and took stock before she attempted to cross the pile of slush that had collected next to the curb. Ribeira Chà's sign was only partially lit because one of the fluorescent bulbs illuminating the sign had burnt out. The two extravagant blue hydrangeas painted next to the name — a reminder of the *hortensias* that grew in tall hedges on the Azorean island of São Miguel where Rosa and Manny came from — were dark. Rosa loved the flowers; she embroidered them on tablecloths and scarves to sell at bazaars, and Manny's family had ordered two big ones to decorate the store when it opened six years before. The plants, Louise also knew, had died, all too symbolically, halfway through the summer.

Now she waved at Manny, trying to catch his attention, but he and the man were looking at the covered-up window, talking about concerns that were lost in the street noise.

Frédéric joined her and helped her step over the melting snow to the sidewalk. "Let me handle this," she said.

Frédéric might have said something, but Manny looked over and saw them. "Madame Brossard," he said. "I didn't know you'd come yourself, I should have telephoned."

"No," she said, "you didn't expect I'd go back on my word, did you? I came as soon as I could. You know my cousin, Frédéric?" She made the introduction and Frédéric held out his hand to Manny. The other man put his hands in his pockets, as if to prevent them from being more cordial than he wanted them to be.

Louise took the envelope with the cash out of her pocket — she'd counted it out and prepared it in the taxi while she waited for Frédéric to finish at the liquor store. "This should cover it," she said. "If there's any left over, use it on something to cheer your spirits. It must be worrying, having the windows broken like that."

"Thank you, but ..." Manny began.

"That won't be necessary," the other man interrupted. "Mr. Da Silva and I have worked out an arrangement."

Louise looked at Manny, who didn't meet her eye. Maybe this man was an investor, or a member of the family who had finally been prevailed upon to help out. Or perhaps — and her heart jumped at this possibility — the man was the father of the kid who broke the window.

Boys who get caught doing stupid things can gain a lot from the experience. Sylvain was a case in point, even though she still shivered when she remembered that dreadful fall when he and his friends — a half-dozen boys who played sword and sorcery games — stole the chalice from Sainte-Anne-d'Outremont. Thomas had insisted that Sylvain change schools and it turned out better than she expected; the academic standard wasn't as good, perhaps, but he met several decent kids. Like Benjamin, the boy whose father was massacred in Rwanda.

Remembering, Louise turned to the man with Manny. "Do you know anything about what happened to the window?" she asked. "Who did it? Or why? I mean, perhaps someone wants to make restitution." She could imagine what a father might be feeling if he were covering for his son; she was about to suggest that an apology would go a long way, but the man laughed.

"Who knows? The way the world is these days, you never know."

The way the world is these days. Indeed, one never knew. "But the guilty parties could pay for the damage," she said. That's what they'd insisted Sylvain and his friends do. That had helped.

Again, the man laughed. "Them directly? Hardly likely."

"So then you'll need the advance," Louise said, turning back to Manny with her arm extended, envelope in hand. "Have you made arrangements to have the work done tonight, or will you have to wait until the morning?"

The man reached out to touch Louise's arm. "It won't be necessary," he said.

Louise looked at him, pulling her arm away. "This is none of your business. It is between Mr. Da Silva, his wife and me," she said, taking care to say the words clearly. There were times when her convent school accent gave weight to what she said.

Manny did not move to take the money. He looked from Louise to the man and back again.

"Mr. Da Silva and I have an arrangement," the man repeated.

Louise hesitated. There was something else going on. "In that case, I will leave the money with Madame Da Silva," she said. "It is only her due, anyway. She is no part of any 'arrangement.'" She turned away and walked the ten feet to the door of the stairway leading to the Da Silvas' apartment above the store. "Frédéric," she said. "I don't think I'm up to climbing those stairs now. Would you take the money up to Rosa?" Then, as Frédéric took the envelope and rang the doorbell, she said to Manny. "This has been a difficult day."

He nodded, but didn't say anything until it seemed he suddenly remembered about Thomas. "Oh yes, Monsieur Brossard," he looked a little flustered, as if he were embarrassed for not asking sooner. "Rosa told me. Is there any news?"

She shook her head, and then stood at the bottom of the stairs silently as she waited for Frédéric to come down. Better to be calmly dignified than to get involved in telling what little she knew in front of this strangely menacing little man in the Kanuk coat. She even refused to look around when a small truck from a glass company pulled up. When Frédéric came back downstairs, she nodded once in the direction of Manny, but said nothing to the other man, who was already talking to the men from the glass company.

Neither she nor Frédéric spoke until they had traversed the two blocks that lay between the Ribeira Chà and Saint-Michel-de-Mile-End. As Frédéric took Louise's arm to help her climb the still snowy steps to the church, he said, "There is trouble there, bigger trouble than I would have imagined."

Louise shook her head in agreement, but she did not want to talk anymore until she had prayed for Thomas.

When Nzosaba came back, he was smiling and jiggling his keys. "Have you ordered?" he asked Thomas. "They were telling me that they've just obtained a *capitaine,* a big fish from the lake. The fishermen are not supposed to be out, for security reasons, but someone was able to land this one." He laughed. "We shouldn't ask too closely after its provenance, but I heartily recommend it."

Thomas smiled and nodded. He was very hungry, and the wine he'd drunk was beginning to go to his head. "Sounds very good," he said. "But would it be possible to have something right away? Bread, perhaps? Or a banana or two, if there isn't any bread?" They might not have bread; Thomas remembered what the hotel manager said about the scarcity of flour. But he didn't want anything that wasn't cooked or that he couldn't peel himself. Another thing he had not appreciated when he travelled as a government minister was that an aide had always been there to make sure that what he ate and drank was wholesome. To live here as an ordinary person would be tiring, always being on guard about the food and water, even in times when you didn't have to worry about the politics.

"Of course," Nzosaba said. "Just a moment, I'll see to it." He disappeared into the kitchen area and Thomas was left once again to look out at the lake. The storm appeared to be over but Thomas saw no sign of anyone along the shore. Tall grass grew all the way to the water's edge, there was no intertidal zone here, no sign that the water level ever changed very much. The commercial part of town seemed to be built on somewhat higher ground, in a flat area that spread back toward the hills, but trees grew near the water, and there were a few houses down here. Nowhere had he seen the kind of banks where there was so much seasonal fluctuation, where waves at high water undermine the shoreline regularly.

Lake Tanganyika and the other African Great Lakes — Malawi, Kivu, Victoria, Turkana and the dry lakes further north — lie in the great cracks and craters that opened as the never-ceasing, unstoppable forces of movement within the earth's crust split the continent apart. They had been there before humans started walking on two legs, and in all likelihood they'll be there after all human life has vanished. A thought which put things in perspective, Thomas realized. Those television news shots of bodies floating in Lake Kivu after the genocide in Rwanda had to be placed next to those of Mount Nyiragongo erupting — at the same moment a spasm of human violence accompanied in time, but not in causality, with a spasm of the earth. Thomas had seen the pictures, felt the connection, remembered thinking that he should file away the extraordinary coincidence to reflect on. So far, he had not done that.

One of the waitresses brought over a small plate with three two-inch long bananas. Her very black fingers shone against the white of the dish, but the inside of her palm was nearly the same colour as that of Thomas's. As if she'd been dipped in chocolate, Thomas thought. Suddenly, he saw himself licking off the chocolate, tasted it even, sweet and rich, dripping with pleasure.

He smiled at her and at himself. He was not a man of limited imag-
ination, nor one who could get by without women. After the election
defeat, he'd missed the lovely young receptionists, the charming
interns, the raspy-voiced reporter, the hostess at the Italian restaurant
on Albert Street. At first, he thought the loss of this galaxy of sexual
possibilities would be the one that cut the deepest, would be even
harder to bear than the indifference which he expected once he was
out of office. Louise had understood that, though. Without saying a
word about what he might want, might need, she made a point of
being there for him in the long, boring afternoons when he missed the
pulse of power the most. She had waited for him with the curtains
closed, so he did not see her as much as feel her flesh, soft and sweet.
She was ready to play any game he desired, she was more attuned to
him than she ever had been.

There was more to her than her availability during that time,
however. She began to think of his future long before he could, when
he was still circling round the ugly fact of defeat. She came up with a
plan for a little consulting firm; she pointed out that he had excellent
credentials and training, even if they were gained years ago. People
still liked him, too. He was constantly being stopped on the street by
old ladies and shopkeepers who told him to "wait until next time," but
Louise said that wasn't enough. He could not afford to wait if there
were to be a next time.

She also put a good spin on the fact that he hadn't been offered a
post by one of the people he used to deal with, especially when so
many of his cabinet colleagues and the PM himself had landed on
their feet in good jobs. She said it showed he had principles.

"They were all looking out for themselves at the end," she told him
as he fussed with his briefcase, getting ready to go downtown on the
bus for a meeting he hoped would be the first of many with managers
of a cable company who wanted his advice. She was sitting at the
breakfast table in her violet velour dressing gown, her hair curling
around her face, the tops of her white breasts showing where the

dressing gown fell open. She wore it a lot lately when he was around because she knew he liked the suggestion of availability, of passion, it wrapped her in. The invitation this morning would have to wait. She rustled the newspapers spread out in front of her, waiting for her to study over coffee after he left.

"You knew what was happening, but you didn't really get involved," she told him once again. "When people started asking questions about Mulroney and those helicopter contracts, no one, I mean no one, mentioned your name. All you did was worry about doing a good job. Now you've got to decide what your next one will be."

He hoped so. He remembered how furious she was when he paraded her before the Oerlikon family. He was grateful all over again for the way she'd allowed him to use her then.

As he stood on the 80 bus as it lurched down Park Avenue, he thought about what she said he should do now. He was so absorbed that he didn't look out the window until the driver honked the horn and the bus stopped. Men were digging up the road to make bus lanes, and even though the morning rush hour was over, traffic was snarled. Thomas heard heavy machinery whipped into life. He did not know, as the bus slowly inched its way past the backhoe and the jackhammers, that this roadwork was what Louise was looking for.

Nor did she, until she called the Ribeira Chà, looking for Rosa, and heard from Manny about the reaction to the changes on Park Avenue. The plan was to make a traffic lane in the middle, which would switch direction at rush hour, speeding cars from the outer suburbs downtown and back. The work was going slowly because the first crews discovered that trolley rails, supposedly removed forty years before, still lay under the asphalt. It was a mess that would last several months, and people in the neighbourhood were not at all pleased.

Louise made several more telephone calls in order to measure the depth of dissatisfaction. "I think mayor would be a good follow-up act," she told Thomas when he arrived home.

Mayor? Being mayor would be a comedown for a whiz kid like him, even if Montreal was the country's second biggest city. But he listened to her because the meeting that morning had been disappointing. Just exactly what the cable people wanted from him remained unclear, although he was sure they wanted to use his old contacts more than his talents. That depressed him.

As soon as he walked in the door, however, Louise was eager to talk about a plan. About what he had to offer. About the municipal election three years away. There was more than enough time to build a campaign, she said, and she had an issue on which to start to build one.

He laughed when she explained. She couldn't be serious. This was silly, a non-issue, and — although he couldn't bring himself to say it — a terrible comedown for somebody who'd been in the big leagues. Municipal infrastructure — what was that? Thomas had always been concerned with more important things — technological development, foreign markets, big treaties and trade. Besides, it seemed to him that whatever could move people around faster in a city was to be desired.

"No, no, no," Louise said. "The plan attacks the very core of the city. The street will become a highway. School children will have a hard time crossing, the elderly will be trapped and the merchants will suffer because parking will be reduced. All so that people can get from the suburbs to downtown in five minutes less than now. This is no way to build a vibrant, people-friendly city. Take on this issue and you've staked out an important field for action."

She was quoting someone, Thomas was sure, she had that tone of voice. He stood, looking out the window at the end of the hall that ran the length of the first floor. Winter had arrived early and the first snow of the season fell softly outside.

He put his forehead and forearms against the window, feeling the coolness in the hollow by the wrist, where the blood vessels lie close to the surface.

Louise was continuing. "They're waiting for a leader," she said. "They're waiting for you."

He turned around so he could look at her. She was serious, her round face blank, the way it turned when she wanted to emphasize the importance of what she was saying. But who cares about bus lanes? Thomas thought, afraid he was going to laugh. The last project he was in charge of was the rewrite of intellectual property laws. For a long time, he'd been the only member of parliament who had any idea what computers would mean for communications, who suspected the impact the Information Age would have on the conduct of business and the organization of work. At one point, he even gave little seminars at lunchtime on Wednesdays for his caucus colleagues who were frightened by the very concept of computers, but had begun to think they should know more. Information systems, computer infrastructure, industrial processes, trade secrets — these were things that mattered. So did economic development, foreign exchange, raising the standard of living. And money, never forget how money matters. Bus lanes didn't.

"Bus lanes," he said out loud.

Louise stopped. Her cheeks were pink, the corner of her mouth twitching just a little, but she didn't speak at once. He could feel her round eyes watching him, with the iris suddenly shaded dark. He knew that she meant business, but he was not prepared for what she said.

"All right. Laugh. But where else are you going to find people who want to work with you and a cause that will get you media space for so little trouble?"

She paused and waited for him to answer. When he didn't, she went on, in English this time, to make a point.

"My dear, you are a loser. And losers, like beggars, can't be choosers."

Loser. Not a word she had ever used before in French or English. It was as if she had taken her soft, smooth hand and struck him right across his face. She repeated the word to underline her point — "Loser."

The wind rattled the windows and blew the wet snow against the glass. Thomas knew that she was right, as she so often was. He was angry that she had said it.

She remained calm, even though he raged at her. "They are expecting you tonight," she said. "There is a meeting to plan the first demonstration."

By the time Thomas walked over to the café and the meeting, the snow had stopped. The heavy equipment was still parked on Park Avenue. The trenches dug to rip out the old tramway rails were full of melting snow. Traffic in each direction was reduced to one lane, although no one seemed to be out on this wet night. Thomas walked quickly; he never liked to enter a hall alone, and he missed his old assistant.

One of the Greek men who always wanted to talk shop greeted him at the door, and so he was passed along from handshake to handshake. By the time he reached the front and turned around, he knew that Louise had won.

What he felt was not unlike sexual excitement. He sensed the electrical charge gather around him, and felt he almost glowed with energy. The others saw it too and reacted, drawn toward him the way iron filings jump toward the poles of an electromagnet. He did not stop to think; he stood in front of the crowd, he smiled, he listened to the introduction. He adjusted his cuffs, he braced his feet, he began to talk. He knew they would follow him, power surrounded him. He was as alive as he ever would be in his life. This was the ultimate seduction of politics, the unnamed thing he had not expected when he started his political life and discovered only after he had struggled with stage fright at his first electoral meetings. It was the pleasure that he missed more than anything else.

On the way home, he regretted it all, though. The whole cause was small potatoes, not worth his effort, beneath his dignity. Certainly there were more things than this that he could do. He was not washed up; he was the same man he'd been before the election. He had so much to give. The wind was blowing streams of clouds across the moon. The temperature was dropping far below freezing. Thomas shivered; the coat he wore was too light for the change in temperature, just as the cause he had found himself championing was too light for the effort.

Louise, however, was delighted at what had happened. She had heard already, one of the Greek men had telephoned to say how Thomas had swept the crowd off its feet.

She met him at the door, wearing the velour dressing gown, and of course he knew what she was expecting — she understood so well the connection between sex and politics. It had been she, after all, who had offered her body all those afternoons in part as a substitute solace. Yet this evening, when she stepped toward him as they stood at the bottom of the stairs, he did not automatically rise to meet her. In order to please her, if not himself, he put his hand on her silky shoulder more than a little reluctantly, but the rest followed, of course. As at the meeting, he could not help himself once he began.

His former assistant called two days later. "What's this I hear about some crackpot protest against the transit commission? Were you out of your mind? Quick and easy transportation is important."

Thomas was the first to agree, so he launched into a long explanation. This particular plan was ill thought out, the impossibility of the traffic, the lack of parking, the death of a neighbourhood.

His old colleague interrupted him — the cable people didn't understand. Could he tell them that Thomas had been hired to help out, that this was a consulting job too? Otherwise, it looked just so small-time.

Thomas let the question, the accusation, hang in the air for a moment. Then he invented, borrowing from what Louise had told him, from what he heard at the meeting. "No," he said, "this is just another example of the incompetence of the present municipal administration. Look at the business with the tramway rails — nobody knew they hadn't been removed, even though somebody got paid for doing it. This is a matter of principle, of good government. This," he said without thinking, "is a new crusade."

So they had a demonstration, and because Park Avenue was the route the television news teams took to get anywhere, Thomas was on the six o'clock news and the local segment after the national news later in the evening. The current city government grumbled and Louise beamed at the good publicity.

The next morning, as they were sitting over coffee, one of the federal party boys called. He wanted to know how much Thomas knew about the computer services contract his ministry had awarded two years ago. "Not much," Thomas said. "Toward the end there, so much was going on that I didn't read everything line by line. That's what you have civil servants for. Everybody knows that." |127

"Not everybody does," the man said. "The downtown real-estate people are very upset about the bus lane business, not to mention the boys who had the contracts for the last road work." He paused to let that sink in. "And somebody's got hold of a report about the support you gave for the high-tech centre in Hull," he said. "It's a report that could be interpreted many ways. Land flips as bad as the Oerlikon business, leases on buildings, all that kind of thing. People are remembering ..."

"The real-estate people are fools," Thomas protested. "The volume of traffic moved on Park Avenue in a morning won't fill up half the office space in one tower and they've got a dozen empty buildings. If they think they're going to get out of this never-ending recession with the shirts on their backs, they're sadly mistaken."

"Doesn't matter, doesn't matter," the man said. "They say, watch out. They say there was funny business over Oerlikon. They say you're a loser, and people are dangerous when they're losers."

"Loser." There it was again.

But dangerous was more interesting. Thomas liked that, when he said the word to himself he felt the same tingling in his hands that he did before he addressed a crowd. His heart pumped harder, he felt the campaigner's smile spread across his face. "We'll show them who's a loser," he said to Louise.

Then on Sunday, Thomas went to Mass at Saint-Michel-de-Mile-End with her. They left the house early, so she would have time to walk at her own pace, a pace that had become slower as she grew larger.

Thomas saw the photographer on the corner right away, although Louise didn't. Not that Thomas minded; he was used to photographers. He even smiled his campaign smile in the man's direction. Then he flashed it at the other church-goers when he and Louise slowly climbed the church stairs.

Louise leaned on his arm. She paused halfway up the dozen steps, placing her hand on her side. Rosa was beside her. They were laughing, but Thomas wasn't paying enough attention to hear what was funny.

Then someone — the photographer, Thomas thought afterwards — lobbed a tennis ball toward them. He didn't throw it hard enough to hurt; the whole business was almost an accident, what one might expect if boys had been playing street hockey nearby. The ball hit Louise on her shoulder and she twisted sharply away, shocked by the blow, no matter how inconsequential.

She grabbed for Thomas as she lost balance. He reached out to catch her, but instead of her elbow he found his hand filled with the softness of her breast. He tried to get a grip on the unresisting flesh, but that only made her scream. The other church-goers turned toward them. The photographer was taking pictures.

In a minute it was over. Thomas shifted his grip, the woman on Louise's other side helped steady her so she did not fall. As if by agreement, they said nothing more about the incident. Thomas hoped that it would not make it harder to get Louise out of the house in the future.

The picture of Thomas did not appear in the newspaper. Instead, it was passed from hand to hand among the city beat journalists and then, later, among the people behind the demonstrations. In it, the woman's face is not visible, only her carefully arranged hair, her huge body. There was no way of knowing it was Louise, not that many people outside of the neighbourhood or the Catholic community knew what she looked like. What was apparent was the look on Thomas's face and the way his hand was grabbing her breast; lust for an enormous woman. It was the kind of picture that gets pinned up in newspaper darkrooms for caption contests. The butt of jokes. Laughable. A way to make a man look ridiculous.

Or, alternatively and equally damning, an Orthodox Jew — and there were a sizable number living in the neighbourhood — might jump to the conclusion that the woman was one of the many heavy, bewigged Hasidic women and think that the man in the photo was a violator of chaste Jewish women.

The damage took a while to be felt. Louise heard nothing about the photo when she telephoned her contacts. Several assured her they'd be there at the next demonstration on the following Thursday, so when it snowed hard that day, they both attributed the small turnout to the weather and nothing else. Thomas did not speak to the crowd; there was no crowd. The Greek men shook his hand, but they didn't hang around to talk.

Then a man said something a couple of others laughed at. Thomas didn't hear exactly what the remark was, nor was he sure it was directed at him. Nevertheless, he felt the hairs on the back of his neck rise and he shivered. Someone had walked over his grave.

The man from the party called the next day. "Louise isn't listening in, is she?" he asked.

Thomas's first thought was to tell him that he ought to be careful, that Louise had always been his best advisor, but then he felt that shiver run down his back again. "She's not listening," he said simply. "What is it that you don't want her to know?"

There was silence at the other end of the line, and Thomas tapped a rhythm on the wall with his middle finger.

Louise passed the doorway and looked in. She carried a tray with five African violet plants on it, on her way to the garden room. Thomas noticed the plants looked wilted, but he took care not to look at her face. He did not want to invite a comment about what he was saying.

His finger tapped away, as if the rhythm came from outside his body, from a force that he would have trouble recognizing or naming.

Still, the man said nothing. Thomas could hear breathing, he thought he might even hear the other's sweat dripping were he to hold his own breath.

Then the man began. "Brace yourself. This isn't going to be sweet." He went on to explain about the photo and the remarks and the serious questions being asked about a man who appeared to be feeling up a woman, maybe even a Hasidic woman.

The urban village, Thomas thought. The drums were beating. But aloud he said, as he had to, "Who cares? It's not true. I'll just deny it."

"What?" Louise said, coming back into the room without the plants. "Deny what?" she asked. She stood there watching for a moment, while Thomas tried to decide what he should claim to deny. Before he could, she went to pick up the extension in the next room.

The party man was saying, "But not everyone knows that your wife is such a big, fat woman."

This was not the first time she had heard that, he was sure. But until now, except for the friend of Richard's years ago who had stood in the entry and screamed at the boy that his mother was as fat and dirty as a pig, she had been safe in her own home.

From where he was standing, Thomas could not see her face, and he tried to judge from the set of her shoulders what she was feeling. He knew he must decide if he wanted to continue.

"Who has the negatives now? Do you know who had them made?" Thomas asked.

"The real-estate guys. But it's not the picture that's important, you know, it's what will come next ..."

"But I don't know. I want specifics," he said. Louise was still clutching the telephone, he saw. Only her hand, turning white with concentration, indicated how upset she was.

"There are other things they might do," he said. "They're going to bring up that business about the land deal in Hull, about Oerlikon. They say that the business with the picture was just a warning."

"How do you know all this?" Louise screamed into the receiver.

The man hung up.

Louise dropped the telephone and turned around to look at Thomas through the open door. Her face was drained of colour. "Big, fat woman," she repeated.

"Louise," Thomas began, moving toward her. "He doesn't appreciate you. None of them do." |131|

"No," she said. She pushed past him and hurried to the front of the house, to the stairs which she climbed without stopping. Thomas would have followed her, but he was afraid that if he did, she would try to move faster, and that if she moved faster, her heart would break.

His own heart beat heavily in his chest. There was indeed a small problem, a little irregularity about the computer contracts, he knew. He had forgotten, he hadn't paid attention. He had so many other things to think about, so many meetings, so many times when he was drunk on the crowd. When he'd started out, detail work had been his strong point, his reputation was built on it, but details had become things others were supposed to take care of. As for Oerlikon, well, there was no denying that he'd been pressured about the land flip and those contracts. He'd had to drag Louise into it.

Upstairs, she cried. He could follow her, tell her that it didn't matter, that he loved her anyway. Right then, he was just a man alone in his kitchen with the snow falling outside. He was alone with the knowledge that he had no future. He was a loser, and losers have few safe places.

The phone rang. For a moment, he was paralyzed with fear, and when he overcame his paralysis to pick up the receiver again, he heard that Louise was already there.

"This is his wife," she was saying. Her voice was almost steady; to someone who did not know her well, the tears she had been shedding moments ago would be undetectable. "There will be a statement in due time," she said. "Thomas Brossard is a man of honour. Thomas Brossard always answers his critics."

The words stayed with him long after he carefully, quietly hung up the receiver. They kept him going during the following months as the mayoral campaign unfolded. In light of them, his reaction when the campaign failed was even more inexcusable.

As he sat, eating the bananas on the shores of Lake Tanganyika, he thought to himself, yes, I must find her wild African violets.

Wednesday, March 19, 1997
Mile End, Montreal, Quebec
Louise

The little light on the answering machine was blinking when Louise and Frédéric walked back into the house.

"No," he said, before she could pick up the telephone. "No, we order dinner first, then you can see who's called. You need something more to eat than oysters and crackers." He was pawing through the little pile of flyers from takeout places. "Souvlaki pita with Greek salad," he said. "We'll have gin and tonics before and some of Thomas's good red during."

She let him call — there was no point in fighting him, she was hungry, she felt like she might dissolve if she didn't eat something substantial, and the idea of a drink pleased her enormously. As soon as he had finished, however, she was punching in the numbers to retrieve the messages.

Nothing from Richard and Anh. She looked at the clock — it was probably still too early for them to be home, they always worked such late hours, even though Anh's baby was due in three months. Nothing from Marielle either, but that was also predictable — she was on call and probably too busy to even check her personal messages. Nothing from Sylvain, but Louise had figured that it would take at least six or seven hours for the message to make its way to him, wherever that was. And nothing from Witness International, which was very disappointing. They should have checked back with her at the end of the business day to say that they did or did not have anything new.

There was only one message, and Louise felt both fury and hope flood over her when she heard it. "Louise, it's Brian here," it began. "What's this I hear about Tom walking out on you?" The former prime minister gave his trademark laugh. "No, sorry, just joking. What I mean to say is that I got wind of what has happened to Tom and I want you to know that if there is anything to do, just let me know. All right? It's understood? And Mila sends her love."

"Did you call Mulroney?" Louise asked Frédéric when she'd listened to the message twice. His number was in the book she'd asked him to call from, she hadn't thought to tell him not to.

"No, I just talked to his former assistant, the one who's got all those contacts in Africa. But that's the kind of thing Mulroney does, isn't it? Always keeps in touch," Frédéric said.

"He's supposed to," she said. "But Thomas hasn't heard from him since the election. And love from Mila! I haven't seen her in what? Six or seven years." Since that awful time at the museum, at the opening of the Oerlikon-Bührle exhibit.

Frédéric was laughing. "Mulroney hasn't taken Thomas to lunch at the Mas des Oliviers, or wherever he makes his power deals now? Well, I hear the food there isn't what it used to be. But look my dear," he paused and took her hand, "you shouldn't be so dismissive of Mulroney's interest. You may need all the help you can get."

She decided she didn't want to comment on that possibility. There were other things to think about too. The clock said seven thirty. The food would be arriving momentarily but she already wanted a drink, she would almost say she deserved a drink. "There's an eight hour difference in time, so what does that make it in Burundi, the middle of the night?" she asked as she carried the dishes from the cupboard and began to set the table. She placed the wine glasses on the table next to the tumblers for gin and tonics. "We aren't going to hear anything directly from there for several hours, I imagine. We probably couldn't even raise anyone at the nearest Canadian embassy at this hour."

"That's Nairobi?"

She nodded. "So I want something to eat. I want something to drink. I think I may even want enough to drink that I go to sleep sitting up, because I don't think I'll be able to sleep otherwise."

She stood aside to let Frédéric start mixing drinks. "If you want a pill to help you sleep, I can get you that," he said, before he handed her the glass. "But if you do, don't drink too much."

She took a gulp and smiled at him. "All we need is for me to overdose."

"Indeed. Chin chin," he added, saluting her with his glass.

They ate in the kitchen, flipping channels back and forth on the little television from the French to the English twenty-four hour news channels. After the gin, Frédéric opened a 1993 Pomerol that he found in Thomas's wine cabinet in the basement.

"The year that the trouble began in Burundi," he said, looking at the label when they were half through the bottle.

"Same year as the election defeat," Louise said. "And to think, I thought at the time that Thomas would be safer after that."

"Safer?"

"You know, away from all that temptation, all those contracts. He is such an honest man, but ..." She let her voice trail off, and then added, smiling, as if it were important to make light of this part, "And the women. I figured there were fewer women to be jealous of, that he'd be safe from that kind of temptation, too."

Frédéric did not answer but sat, holding his glass up to the light, admiring the play of colours in the wine. "There's another bottle. I'd like some more," he said finally.

Louise nodded, and after he left to get the bottle in the basement, she picked up a french fry in her fingers. As she contemplated it, she realized that if she found this bit of soggy potato worth looking at carefully, she didn't need anything more to drink. Then, when the phone rang, she knocked over her glass, spilling the little wine she had left into her plate. "Hello," she said, hoping to hear one of the children, the man from Witness International, one of Thomas's old cronies with news. She squared her shoulders, willing herself not to sound drunk.

"Madame Brossard," Rosa said on the other end of the line. "Thank you so much, thank you, thank you."

I don't want to worry about your problems Rosa, Louise thought. But she said, "Oh Rosa, it was nothing, really." She struggled to keep her tone light, to distance her disappointment. "It's money you earned, or you will earn, anyway. If it helps you to have it early, well I'm glad."

"But you don't understand," Rosa said. "It's more than just the advance, it's that you did it so quickly. Because you brought it over when you did, maybe Manny will be all right."

"I hope so my dear, I sincerely hope so." But she doubted that what was wrong with Manny and the Ribeira Chà could be fixed by replacing broken windows. Doing that was going to take much more, would take a miracle. "He's going to be open tomorrow?" she asked. Frédéric appeared from the basement, waving a wine bottle in each hand. When he looked quizzically at her, she mouthed, "Rosa."

"Yes, yes," Rosa said. "The windows are fixed and it will be business as usual. And he's going to meet them at Central Market tomorrow morning, so he can insist that he won't need their help."

"Who's they?" Louise asked. Through the fog of the wine, the worry and her growing annoyance at the insinuation of Rosa and her problems into her life, she began to pick up vibrations of something else troubling.

"The men who want to invest in the Chà," Rosa said. "Manny said you met one of them this afternoon."

The little man in the suit and tie who said he and Manny had made an arrangement. The word echoed in her heard after she'd said goodbye and told Frédéric what Rosa had said.

"Protection money," Frédéric said. "Money laundering. Something's going on."

"Yes," Louise said. "Give me some more wine."

Tuesday, March 18, 1997
Bujumbura
Thomas

"African violets? Violets of Usumbura?" Nzosaba asked when Thomas told him what he wanted to do. Nothing but bits of skin from the fish was left on their plates, and a bottle of South African white wine sat empty between them. They had talked about where the rice they'd eaten came from — the flood plain of the Ruzizi — a possible export if peace was ever found. Then Nzosaba had explained the education system — modelled after the Belgian system at the higher levels, but reaching only a small percentage of children because of political instability. When Thomas asked about the prospects for settlement, Nzosaba shook his head and stared out the window.

It was now about 3 p.m. The Club Nautique was empty except for them, and Nzosaba had shaken himself out of his reflection to ask what else Thomas would like to see.

"Violets of Usumbura is one of the names for them, and Bujumbura used to be Usumbura, right?" Thomas said. "So the plants must originally come from somewhere near here. The thing is my wife grows them, and she'd love it if I could bring one back to her from the wild."

Nzosaba pursed his lips and looked down at the plate. Thomas took that to mean exporting plants might present problems, so he went on, "Or, if that would be impossible, if only I could tell her I'd seen them growing naturally, maybe take a picture or two."

The other man considered. He picked up a crust of bread and rolled it between his fingers so that it was reduced to crumbs. Then he looked up. "Where do you think these plants might be found?" he asked.

"I don't know. I was hoping you might have some idea. Does the university have a botany department? Perhaps someone there would know."

"The university," Nzosaba began. "Well, the university has suffered, as have we all. I had a classmate who was most interested in the study of fish, did graduate work in France and in the States, who used to say that Lake Tanganyika held more mysteries and wonders than we could imagine. But after his parents were killed, he decided he could not come back." He picked up the crumbs with the tips of his fingers and then threw them back on his plate. "I am afraid that is the case for far too many of our experts. We didn't have many to begin with, the Belgians were very backward when it came to educating us colonials, and there was not one local man with a university education when we gained our independence. Things are worse now because no one who is trained, who could have a future elsewhere, wants to stay. I should know, I've been trying to run an importing business without anybody who knows anything to help. It's bad enough with the embargo, but that will end, sooner rather than later. The shortage of trained people won't." He looked up from his plate to meet Thomas's eyes. "People want to leave, or at least they want their children to leave."

Yes, Thomas thought, this is what he's been aiming at all day. I shouldn't be surprised. How many people is he speaking for? Does he have specific cases to bring up?

"You know what it is like to get a visa to study abroad? You must first be accepted in a university program and then you have to prove that you won't be a burden on the host country. The Belgians want to see your bank accounts, your stock holdings, they make the student sign a paper saying that he will leave within a two-week period after his courses have finished. Getting a student visa for Canada is easier, but you have to have a temporary resident visa before that. And that's worse than what the Belgians put you through."

Thomas knew that. How many calls had his office received from a constituent whose nephew or brother wanted to come to Montreal to study? Discussions about immigration and refugee policy were staples in cabinet meetings, too.

"You know, I haven't been in office for nearly four years," he stopped Nzosaba from going any further. "I have no influence anywhere at all now, and besides, Canadians officially run an immigration service free of favouritism."

"No, no, I wasn't talking about particular cases," Nzosaba protested. "And you may be out of government now, but in Canada that does not mean much, does it? You have elections and people win or lose, and sometimes win again. Besides, you know people, and we want to make sure the word is spread."

"What word?" Thomas said before he thought.

"That those who want to escape should be allowed to."

"You're talking refugees, like in Rwanda. Like the people in the camps I'm going to visit."

"I'm talking about people before they become refugees."

Thomas thought of the news footage of the roads filled with people loaded down with bedding, cooking pots and water containers; of all the statistics and events stuffed into the Witness International documents; of the look on the faces of the women in the laundry where they'd taken shelter on Sunday; of the boys chasing the smaller one the day before that.

"I'm talking about people before they are killed," Nzosaba continued. "Burundi and Rwanda are as densely populated as Belgium, and we Tutsis in Bujumbura are surrounded by people who hate us. In the countryside, there are others who the militia would like to shoot on sight. It has gone on so long now, there have been so many killed, that you can't expect people, whoever they are, to show much restraint. Why not let those who can leave, leave?"

"But don't people want to stay here, on their hills? Don't they just want to have some land to call their own? Don't they just want peace? Isn't that what everybody says? Doesn't the country need their expertise? How are you ever going to break out of a mess if everybody with any training leaves?"

"You're right, of course. And given the best of all possible worlds, staying is what I'd want to do. Grow old with the hills behind me and the lake in front of me, with God on my side and a king restored. But it isn't going to happen." He paused again and picked up his glass to drain the two drops that remained. "You know the kingdom of Urundi was never conquered, and our people were never slaves. We kept out the Germans until after the turn of the twentieth century, and we never did let the slave traders operate. That's why our population has always been so high — this is fertile land, this is a region of two harvests a year and rain just when you need it. Starvation was unknown when the Europeans arrived. The Germans called it the land of milk and honey."

He was looking directly at Thomas, who felt he had to say something. "So you all love the land and the cattle who own it," he said finally. He expected Nzosaba to laugh, to allow a little of the intensity of the conversation to leak away.

But Nzosaba did not take it as a joke. "Exactly," he said. "So you can see how difficult things must be if we think of leaving. Now, there are rumours that there is some high-level negotiating going on, that Nelson Mandela is going to start working on a plan for peace and reconciliation. But that's in the future, and the killing goes on. Don't prejudice the lives of people who simply want to escape before a machete is waved in their faces, or a soldier with a rifle lines them up to be shot."

"You're talking about Hutus? Or Tutsis?"

He did not answer immediately. "If you're asking me who is right and who is wrong, who has sinned the most and who has clean hands, I would have to say everyone and no one. If you ask me who I know would like to see me dead, and whom I would kill with my bare hands if we were thrown together in a cavern on a dark night, I could tell you, but I hope you won't ask." He pushed his plate aside and began to brush the crumbs from the table with one side of his hand, and to catch them in his other. "Just do what you can to give us a chance to get out when we must," he said as he clapped his hand together, scattering the crumbs on the floor. Then he folded his hands, his elbows on the table, and turned his head to look out at the lake.

"So," he said. "Forgive me if I have said too much."

Thomas sat, silent, for a few moments. "I have no influence at all anymore," he repeated. "There is little that I can do to help you or your friends." If he were to treat these people properly, he must tell them that. Nevertheless, he felt his heart beat just a little faster at the return of the once familiar feeling that he had influence, that he was important. He had not felt it for such a very long time.

The year before, the first heavy snow came in mid-November — twenty centimetres fell between mid-afternoon and early evening. Thomas did not try to come home for dinner, the entire island of Montreal was frozen in gridlock, the snowplows and salt trucks barely advanced as they struggled to cut trails through the mountains of falling flakes. No problem, he told Louise on the phone, he'd grab a sandwich or a souvlaki in the food court of the building where he was renting office space. Then he'd take the Metro to the meeting. Very easy to do.

By the time he arrived, he was feeling rather good about the way Montreal turned winter into an adventure. Good thoughts for a man who wanted to be mayor, who was aiming to be the city's greatest booster, who was on the comeback trail.

He ducked out of the Metro station and ran across the street to the building where the municipal party executive was meeting. The piles pushed up by the plows were knee-deep at the corner, but he leapt over them with no more trouble than getting snow on his trousers. Just inside the lobby he brushed the snow off, while he waited for the elevator to take him to the third floor offices of the law firm where the municipal party's president was a partner. That was when he began to realize the meeting he was going into had been discussed by many people. Two men were talking behind the door leading to the stairs, their voices loud enough for him to be sure they didn't think they were being overheard. Nevertheless, they tarried a minute before opening the door and coming out into the lobby. A private conversation, one he wasn't expected to hear.

"The strategy is good," one voice said.

"Yeah, they've thought it all out pretty carefully. The candidate profile and the focus group results agree."

"So they're going to go with him? Does he know it yet?"

A laugh. "That's what I'm led to believe."

"And he'll go along with the restraints?"

"That too, they say."

"All right."

The door pushed open and two men in their late thirties surged out, buttoning their coats and pulling on caps. Thomas didn't recognize either of them, but obviously his face was familiar to at least one of them. The man looked surprised, then a little panicked, but he recovered himself. "The Honourable Monsieur Brossard," he said, nodding. "Good evening."

The Honourable sounded good, even though he hadn't been entitled to it for three years. "Good evening to you too, sir," he said.

The other man took a long hard look at Thomas, as if considering, as if he wanted to remember what Thomas looked like at this point in time, as if noting down the circumstances for posterity. Then the pair were gone, out into the whirling snow. Good strategy, Thomas thought to himself, that sounds interesting. He stepped lightly into the elevator when it arrived, confident that the signs were in his favour. Which at first, they seemed to be.

That was the shock of it, really, when he was told the party was picking a younger man, a lawyer without a track record. "But my experience," he remembered trying to say, and the party president saying, "That's just it, Tom."

When the meeting was over — when he was through with the meeting — he plunged outside into the cold and began walking home. The snow had stopped, the sky was clearing and the temperature was dropping fast. Thomas turned up his collar and thrust his hands into his pockets, not realizing until he had walked west on Sainte-Catherine as far as Place des Arts, that he had left his hat behind with the others. They were probably sitting around the table in the lawyers' conference room, with the wood glowing warmly in the indirect lighting, the bottoms of wine glasses leaving circles on the glow. He had his gloves on, and when he turned north up Saint-Urbain, he pulled his hands out of his pockets so he could hold them over his ears. If he walked a block further west, he could take the bus up Park Avenue. But he was not going to take the bus, he did not like taking the bus, cabinet ministers didn't take buses; politicians didn't unless they were surrounded by staff and trying to appear like men of the people.

He didn't have enough money on him for a taxi, though. Louise had sent him off that morning with what they'd agreed was plenty for an ordinary day, but he'd had an extra drink at lunch time, and then the donair kabob that he'd bought had been more than he'd expected. Trashy food-court food.

He was fed up with worrying about cab fare and restaurant meals and people who didn't know strategy from a hole in the ground. He had been three years in purgatory and it was about time for it to end. He could no longer abide what was going on.

As he walked, the difficulties became clearer to him, the challenges before him more maddening. He plowed up the sidewalk, unaware that snow was twenty-five centimetres deep in places, that cars were having trouble stopping, that he was hard to see. His hands grew cold and he stuck them back in his pockets, hunching up his shoulders to try to protect his ears. He stepped aside automatically when a snow-clearing sidewalk tractor sped toward him. He didn't pause at corners, but strode across streets, unaware that there was anyone else, driver or pedestrian, on the road.

At what point did his anger transfer to Louise? Halfway up Saint-Urbain, maybe when he decided that he had no real desire to pursue her plan. It had been her plan, no doubt about it. She was responsible; she was the one who had suggested he do this and that. At the time he had given her credit for being concerned about him, for being proud of him, for having confidence in what he could do. Now, however, it was beginning to look to him as if she had pulled the strings for her own pleasure. She had set him up. She was responsible for the humiliation that he had just suffered.

It was at this point that he arrived at the house, and to his later regret, threw open the door and stormed down the hall, across the kitchen and into the garden room, where Louise stood, surrounded by her plants.

Five months later and half a world away, Nzosaba looked at the water of Lake Tanganyika. "So," he said, turning back to Thomas, a smile on his handsome face. "You want to go looking for some flowers."

Wednesday, March 19, 1997
Mile End, Montreal, Quebec
Louise

There was no news from Burundi, no news from any part of Africa on any of the programs that Louise could get as she flipped through the channels. She had another open bottle of Pomerol in front of her, but Frédéric had switched to Thomas's scotch. The souvlaki was gone, it was dark outside. Frédéric announced that he was going to spend the night.

"You need someone to keep you company here tonight," he said. "I'll call home and say that I'm staying. Richard's room is the guest room now, isn't it?"

Louise did not comment on the fact that Frédéric now had someone waiting for him to come back. Nor did she tell him that she had not decided which bedroom was the guest room, although of the three children's rooms, Richard's was the least littered with the residue of former lives. At about nine o'clock, Marielle finally telephoned and offered to come down from Quebec the next day when she was no longer on call. "I can swing it, I've got seventy-two hours off," she said.

THE VIOLETS OF USAMBARA

Louise said no. "Frédéric is here, Sylvain will turn up." Then before she could stop herself, she said what she hadn't intended to say. "Don't use up any free time that you may have coming to you. I may need you more later."

There was silence on the other end of the line as Marielle considered that. "I see," she said, her voice almost at the point of breaking into tears, "let me talk to Frédéric."

Frédéric said the same things that Louise had said, but Marielle seemed to absorb the facts better.

"Are you okay, Maman?" she said when Frédéric handed the receiver back to Louise. "I'll go light a candle in the chapel as soon as I get off the phone, and I'll call in the morning, but you've got to promise me that you'll call first if there's any news."

"Of course, of course," Louise agreed, but she couldn't say anything more. She'd recovered a bit by the time Richard called, but she knew enough to pass the phone to Frédéric as soon as her voice began to grow husky with emotion.

An hour or so later, the man from Witness International called, which at first sent Louise's hopes soaring. He had no news, though. "I'm sorry, I'd love to tell you that all is well, but perhaps we'll hear something in a few hours. It will be morning there soon. In the meantime, you should try to get some sleep."

Better said than done, but she went to bed, leaving Frédéric sitting with a fresh scotch on the table by his side. Upstairs, Louise said her rosary and climbed into her big, empty bed. She lay there, listening to the wind outside, wondering what sounds Thomas might be hearing at that moment. Maybe wind in trees, or the morning sounds of a city waking up — cars, buses, children crying, cocks crowing.

Then she was awakening to silence. The wind had died down, there were no faint traffic sounds coming from Park Avenue, no behind-schedule airplanes approaching Dorval. No lights from downstairs shone up the landing outside her room. A small rumble came from

Richard's room. Frédéric must be snoring, but that wasn't what had awakened her. There had been something else, a noise of some sort, and now she noticed its absence. She listened, half fearing that what had disturbed her was a kind of psychic message from the other side of the world. Only when she heard the inner front door close, she realized what had awakened her must have been the sound of someone opening the outer door.

Footsteps went to the closet off the front hall as a coat, hat and boots were stowed. Then they continued down the hall to the kitchen. That door shut and she heard no more.

Not a burglar. Burglars didn't carefully take off their boots when they entered a house. Someone with a key, surely. Not Rosa, of course. Rosa had no reason, tonight of all nights, to come over. Not Richard, not Marielle. Maybe Sylvain.

Louise sat up and quickly felt on the floor for her slippers with her bare feet. Then she grabbed the dressing gown she'd put at the end of the bed.

He wasn't in the kitchen when she entered it, even though the kettle had been turned on and was beginning to burble. There was a teapot and cup on the counter next to the stove, too. Then she heard the toilet flush in the basement. He'd gone down to use the bathroom there so he wouldn't disturb her. How considerate he could be when he wanted to, she told herself. He'd grown up.

Frédéric must have tried to clean things up a bit after she'd gone to bed. The Styrofoam containers from dinner had been dumped in the big trash bin, the lid half off. Their wine glasses and empty bottles were lined up on the counter by the sink, with the dirty plates stacked to the side. No sign of the frying pan or cutting board — they must still be outside — but the onion peelings and olive oil bottle had been cleared away.

She leaned forward, her head in her hands. The light hurt her eyes, too big a change from the darkness of her room, too much brightness after more wine than she was used to. Too many worries.

"Maman," Sylvain said when he reached the top of the stairs. "What's going on? The dispatcher said the person who called sounded really strange. I decided to come over as soon as I got back in town."

She told him after she'd hugged him. She did it without breaking down, and then he made tea for both of them as he told her where he'd been. Ten days on the road, all the way to Vancouver and then down to Portland, Oregon, but that afternoon he'd been in the Thousand Islands region of Ontario when the message reached him. He should have stopped. According to his log book he was supposed to have eight hours off before he drove again, but once he received the message, he headed home. "I'll worry about the log in the morning," he said when Louise asked how he could get around the rules.

She looked at the clock — nearly 4 a.m. She remembered the nights she'd nursed him, and his sister and brother before him. She'd never minded a middle of the night feed, when it was just her and the smallest child. She read *Madame Bovary* then, and wondered if Emma would have been less restless if she'd been more involved with her child. She read *War and Peace* and understood why Natasha, lovely quicksilver Natasha, could be so excited at the end of the book over a diaper that no longer showed green baby diarrhea.

She had daydreamed about the great things her babies would do and she tried to figure out just how to get Thomas to live up to his potential. That had been a long time ago.

Sylvain brought her back into the present. "Did you call Papa's sisters, or that place where Grandma is living now? What do his old buddies say about this?"

She looked at him. "We'll call the aunties when we have more news," she said, suddenly a little ashamed she hadn't thought of them or of her own family. Their brothers and sisters couldn't help, though; they were all a good day's journey from Montreal. Her own parents were as fragile as Thomas's mother, who'd been in an institution for two years. "As for Papa's friends, we contacted a few," she said. "Mulroney called."

"Good," he said, "but there are a lot of others — the ambassadors, the ex-ministers, the guys who know everything and everybody."

Louise was about to shake her head. Sylvain didn't know how she'd had to work to get Thomas invited on this mission, but she didn't want to let the boy know just how bad things were. "Maybe I should make another list," she said.

He stood up and went to fetch paper from the breakfast nook. The fax machine rang and began to spit out a message.

"What is it?" she called to him. A note from the Canadian embassy in Nairobi, maybe? Something from someone with contacts at another NGO?

She heard him rip the paper from the machine, and then rip earlier messages off the one which had just came in. "Garbage," he said. "The big office supply store has a special on fax paper and photocopy toner. You want me to toss it?"

She sighed, she should have expected that. "Yes, put it there with the stack we use for scratch paper," she said. Then she remembered that she hadn't looked closely to see what had come in while she was gone. "Is there anything else? I've been away for a few days."

"A couple of things. Mostly looks like ads," he said, glancing quickly at the messages. "They go in the scratch pile too?"

"I'll look at them later," she said. "Just bring me my address book, and we'll see who might help." She looked at the clock again — 4:45 a.m., or early afternoon in Burundi. There might be news soon.

Monday, March 17, 1997
Bujumbura
Thomas

Thomas was back on the hotel terrace, drinking beer and listening to the early evening sounds of birds settling down for the night in the hotel's garden, when Nzosaba called him. He was glad to get the call because Bailey had announced at dinner there was going to be another delay. Gasoline, he'd been promised, had been commandeered for another mission. Just what that was he hadn't been able to determine, but they would have another day of enforced idleness at least. The two others on the team were busy lining up visits to other NGOs at that moment, while Thomas was wondering how best to occupy himself the next day. While he talked to Nzosaba on the telephone, he stood with his back to the bar, looking out across the terrace toward the swimming pool surrounded by the flowering bushes. Flowers — there were so many whose names he didn't know. He should take pictures of them for Louise — she'd recognize them — even if he couldn't find wild African violets.

Nzosaba did not have encouraging news. "I finally was able to contact my friend at the university, but he has no idea where you might look. His field is chemistry, though, so that's not surprising," he said. "Then I asked him to inquire among his colleagues, and the best he came up with was a priest working at a mission school up near Gitega who has done quite a bit of botanizing, and a botanist who is on staff at the university, but who is in France at the moment. Which means, I'm afraid, that there's no one in Bujumbura who could help you."

Thomas murmured his disappointment, but Nzosaba didn't wait for a more articulate reply. "The only place that I can think of where they might grow is up in the nature reserve along the Ruzizi, but it is not a place you want to go. The river is the border with Zaire, you know, and there have been a lot of rebels going back and forth across it."

"Isn't that one of the areas I'm supposed to visit on the mission?" Thomas asked. He wished he had the map that had come in the document packet. He tried to remember what he'd seen from the air as they came in. The airport was on the flood plain before the river met the lake, he seemed to remember.

"Perhaps, I don't know what your itinerary is. Mr. Bailey should know, you'll be travelling as a group, you'll be more or less protected. But individuals shouldn't risk it."

"So you're saying that I should forget about a flower-finding expedition?"

"In essence, yes. Your wife will understand, surely. This is a dangerous country."

Again, Thomas made a noise that could be interpreted in many fashions, but Nzosaba was continuing. "However, I was wondering, should you be free tomorrow evening, if you would join us for dinner."

"Us?" Thomas asked. People whom Nzosaba wanted Thomas to help, without a doubt. How many invitations had Thomas had like this on his trips as a minister? His staff had always fielded the requests for him; he could always say that the person extending the invitation should check with his aide to see if he was free. He didn't have to ask exactly what the parameters for invitations were, he never had to think of how to refuse one politely. He could appear grateful for all invitations, even those it might be wise to decline. Louise had been acting as his social secretary for the last while, but here he was completely on his own. "How very kind of you," he added, remembering that even if he had to refuse, he should be polite.

"Who will we be?" Nzosaba said. "Some of my associates and my sons. We will be dining at my humble residence, and we would be extremely grateful for your presence. We will arrange for your transportation — you needn't worry about travelling after curfew."

Formulas of politeness covering the hope that Thomas might give them real reason to be grateful. He could not see how he could refuse, nor did he want to. It was pleasant, he had to admit, to be considered a man whose favour was worth cultivating.

"We would especially like to talk to you about the way you accommodate losers in Canada."

Thomas laughed with shock. "Losers? You want to talk to me because I lost my election and I'm out of power?"

"No, no. I see I've put it badly. What I mean is, you have elections and people lose, but they don't have to go into exile. You have conflict between groups, but you don't kill each other. We need to learn how ..." He paused and cleared his throat. "This is not a topic of conversation for the telephone. Please join us so we may speak face to face."

They monitor telephone calls here? Well, why not? What country didn't? And what failed politician did not like to be asked his advice and opinion? So he agreed.

The barman had finished washing the last of the glasses in front of him. The smell of iodine-purified water still lingered in the air. Thomas hung up and handed him back the telephone. "Thank you," he said. "Another beer, if you please." Despite Nzosaba's inability to arrange a quest for violets, Thomas felt rather pleased about what the next day might hold.

The barman flipped the cap off a cold bottle of Amstel. "Unfortunately, we do not have many more," he said. "Transport and production have been disrupted off and on for several weeks, and with the blast yesterday, the supplier says we may not get anymore until the end of the week."

Thomas nodded and took a sip. It was good beer, and, most important on an evening like this, cold. "Well," he said. "This should be enough for me for tonight." He leaned against the bar and turned back toward the terrace and the garden. While he had been on the phone, two thin, lovely young women with creamy, chocolate brown skin had come in with a tall man as corpulent as they were slim. He watched the girls laugh while the man finished telling a story.

"Did I hear you sounding disappointed because you will be unable to visit some place you wanted to go?" the barman asked.

Thomas turned around to look at him. He grinned, "I thought it was a standard worldwide that bartenders were discreet."

The man grinned back. "I won't tell anybody else, I was just asking. I'm the soul of discretion. But if you need transport some place, perhaps I can arrange it."

"Of course, of course. Another worldwide standard is that barmen can arrange anything," Thomas said, grinning again.

"I don't know worldwide, but I do know Bujumbura, and I think I probably can help you."

Thomas looked the barman up and down. He'd noticed earlier that the man was a little shorter than most of his customers, but taller than the waiters and the housekeeping staff. Bujumbura was a Tutsi city, the country was Hutu — was it possible that this man had contacts in both camps that could insure a relatively safe trip out of town, contacts that Nzosaba didn't have?

"My friend on the phone was telling me that it would not be prudent to visit the nature reserve along the river," Thomas said. "What do you think?"

154

The man picked up a glass he'd already polished and began to polish it again. "Along the river," he said after a time. "In the Rukoko forest."

Thomas looked at him intently, trying to guess what he was weighing as options. "Rukoko forest? I hadn't heard that name. But yes, along there where the old maps show stands of palm trees. People tell me that there are some untouched corners there where you can find interesting things."

This time the man's response was immediate. "Like what?"

Thomas had not considered what you might find besides African violets, but he now saw that a multitude of contraband might come out of the woods. "Plants," he said quickly. "I don't want any trouble, I'm not trafficking in arms, or children or anything like that."

The barman returned his gaze. Then he smiled again. "I didn't think you were. I was told you were with an NGO, and not all the people who're hooked-up with them are spotless. But you look all right." He put the glass and his towel down on the counter then leaned forward. "So, all you want is a driver who'll take you up to look around in the reserve? Even though there might be a little danger attached? I won't kid you — there are groups of rebels who pass through there, who might not like people who look official coming their way."

Thomas nodded. "I mean, I don't want to do anything foolhardy, but what kind of trouble can I get into if we just stop along the road at a few likely spots and see what I can find?" Then he added, "Would the driver be armed?"

"That could be arranged. It would cost extra."

"How much?" Thomas tried to remember how much in US dollars he had left. Nzosaba had signed for the meal at the Club Nautique. Compliments of the hotel, he said, before Thomas had a chance to see how much the bill came to. Nor had he even looked at the hotel room rates, since Witness International was paying the bill. He had barely touched his cache, really.

The barman considered. "Well, let's say one hundred dollars for the car and driver, fifteen for the gas, fifteen for meals and twenty-five for the extra protection," he figured rapidly on a napkin. "That makes one hundred and fifty-five dollars, plus a ten percent commission for me, so it comes to one hundred and seventy, more or less."

Thomas hesitated — even figuring that prices were rising because of the embargo and the NGOs, who could pay whatever the market could bear, one hundred and seventy dollars sounded like a lot of money.

"I'll have to think about it," Thomas said. He turned his back on the man and looked again at the table where the two handsome women sat.

"You want to be sure you're safe," he heard the barman say. "Well, you can't be safe for anything less."

Thomas took a sip of his beer and wiggled his shoulders, which suddenly seemed stiff, as if they'd been locked in place for too long. The women really were attractive. He watched while they both laughed at their companion's jokes and sipped prettily at their bottles of lemonade, as if they were on display. They were, in fact, Thomas was pretty sure. He'd spent enough time in bars and restaurants late at night to recognize flesh for sale. Not that he indulged himself that way ordinarily. He preferred women he knew socially or through his work, although, if he added up money spent on dinners and the rest, dealing with a professional was less expensive, usually. None of that mattered, though. Louise was his wife, *point à la ligne finale.*

But these were very attractive young women, he had to admit.

"The one in the red dress would cost more than what I am proposing," the barman said. "Just to give you an idea of what the price scale is here. Look at it that way, less than a high-class, guaranteed healthy whore."

"Guaranteed healthy?" Thomas said. "No AIDS?"

"Guaranteed. Look at them — such lovely skin and firm bodies. Although, an intelligent man always uses protection in his affairs of the heart or the body."

"Indeed," Thomas said. "As does an intelligent man who goes exploring." He turned around. "All right," he said. "What time can you get the driver here and how long do you think we should allow for our expedition?"

"He will be here about nine o'clock, and you should be back here by late afternoon," the barman said, picking up the telephone. "I will call immediately. And afterwards, should I take the lady in the red dress another lemonade?"

Thomas nodded.

Thursday, March 20, 1997
Mile End, Montreal, Quebec
Louise

Sylvain left Louise sitting in the kitchen and went to bed just before the sky began to change colour. "I'm sorry Maman, but if I don't crash now, I'll run into some real problems down the line," he said. "All that travel catches up with you."

He leaned over to kiss her on the cheek. "Just call if you need anything, although you may have to call pretty loudly," he said.

"If you remember, I'm pretty good at that," she said, and wrapped her arm around his waist so she could pull him close. He smelled of cigarette smoke and sweat, although he had not lit up a cigarette since he arrived. Maybe he could take things or leave them, as he always insisted when he was a little younger. Well, at least it was tobacco he smelled like and not marijuana.

He laughed and hugged her back. "No comment," he said. "You ought to get some sleep too."

She nodded, but she knew she wouldn't be able to go back to sleep. It would be afternoon in Bujumbura. If there was going to be news today it should be on its way shortly.

She could see the sky beginning to lighten above the house next door through the garden room windows. This was an hour that she liked. There had been nights when the children were little and she'd got up to attend to someone's bad dream or restless sleep, when she would sit calmly by herself for a while afterward, pleased that she had no reason to feel guilty about not attending to the many jobs that must be done. Then after they'd reached late adolescence, there had been nights when she'd awaken shortly after the hour they were due home. She would get up and pad around the house barefoot, checking to see that their bedroom doors were closed, that their boots were by the front door, that they had safely returned from whatever foolishness might have tempted them that evening. Now she no longer woke wondering if they were all right, but she still enjoyed this time of day when, for whatever reason, she found herself contemplating the dawn.

She went into the garden room to see the first rays of sun hit the tall apartment building to the southeast. Its top floors were just visible above the roofs of the houses immediately next to their's. Sometimes at this hour after a storm, the wind whipped plumes of snow off the building's roof, sending the snow flying into the air like a silk scarf. The garden room windows were steamed up a little, however, so she saw the light outside well but not the fine detail of the morning.

The windows.

The windows that Thomas had broken last November. That she had been trying not to think about all afternoon and evening, despite the drama at the Ribeira Chà. The anger and nausea that she had worked so hard to control thrust itself forward.

At the time, she had told herself that she understood how Thomas felt when the politicos turned him down, when they said they wanted a younger, hipper, newer candidate for mayor. It might be the second biggest city in the country, but it still was only mayor, and they didn't want him, even for that. He'd been pushed too far, they had been terribly cruel.

Once he calmed down, he helped her bring in the plants that stood on the shelves along the windows. He blocked the broken glass with layers of plastic taped to the frame and called a glazier. It took all the authority that he'd learned in government, but he succeeded in demanding that the man come immediately to make repairs, despite the hour, despite the storm. There had been ten or fifteen minutes, however, when the temperature plummeted from summertime to deepest winter. Minus fifeen. Cold enough to freeze anything from East Africa. Cold enough to kill her plants.

The windows, broken windows.

For three days she couldn't look at the remaining plants. It took that long to gather her courage so she could examine the limp, dissolving, ice-blasted leaves. Of the fancy ones she had been working on at her bench, a half-dozen survived because they had fallen on the floor, next to the radiator and were spared the worst of the cold. Among them were two double-blossomed plants, which she'd been trying to cross, one purplish red, the other violet.

That pleased her. At least they were saved.

The cross was not one to be advised, some breeders said, because the offspring of double-blossomed plants can produce flowers too heavy for the stems. Louise had long thought this was nonsense. The beauty came in the heaviness, and she could imagine what she might produce if she succeeded — the voluptuousness of the flower, its luxurious excess. She knew that had been part of the attraction from the beginning. She loved this, this playing God, this manipulating destiny.

Furthermore, she'd been working toward this cross for four years. At the beginning, she had carefully chosen flowers on strong stems, then worked toward the double-blossomed traits. Now she was going after colour, a particular purple-red that burned in her mind.

Castration was the next step. Illustrations in books make it appear less sinister, more like cutting flowers for a bouquet; nail scissors poised next to an anther. But what she had to do was take the flower on the plant in which she wanted the seeds to develop and cut away its male parts so that it would not pollinate itself. Cut away the flower's two yellow anthers — two round sacks and a long tube descending from them like the graffiti of the archetypal male.

There was something so comical about a naked man. A boy, a little boy, could be a pleasure to look at. The health, the energy, the round firmness of a small body was as marvellous as the smooth fur of a puppy, the lusciousness of a peach, the taut radiant skin of an apple. | 161

But a naked man ...

Thomas had prepared her for the way one of his legs was smaller than the other, and she had known what to expect about the rest of him. She had read books, she had felt him against her when they kissed. But a naked man, a naked Thomas. The light from the open bathroom door had outlined him that night after they'd been married by the judge in Plattsburgh. The skin on the top of his shoulder had shone palely. He had walked toward her as she lay on the bed, his breath short and raspy, as if he'd been running. He could not run with that thing extended, however, she was sure.

She wanted to laugh, to giggle in embarrassment and confusion at the way he was so intent on what would come next. She did not, though, there was no reason to be embarrassed or ashamed; they were married finally. She had not lied to her parents on the Île d'Orléans for their holiday, she had merely let them assume because she knew they'd accept a pregnant daughter and quick marriage more readily than they would have the real, bureaucratic reason for the haste — that Thomas had just learned that he was going to be called up.

She had not let Thomas enter her, even after they'd told her parents. "Wait," she had said. "We've waited this long, we can wait a bit more." She was that much a good Catholic girl.

And then, after they were married and Frédéric and his friend had left, after she and Thomas had checked into the old inn down by the lakefront, after that first brief sight of Thomas's body outlined in the dim light of their room, she did not look below his shoulders, she waited for him to touch her. That was what she wanted, that was not at all laughable.

His body at that point, at least, had the advantage of being young and thin. It was thicker more than thirty-five years later, the meetings, the lack of exercise showed. Now, when he came to her in their house with the African violets growing in the garden room and the detritus of children and the souvenirs of their years together, he often turned the light off, but out of vanity, not embarrassment. Even in the long, lonely afternoons in the days following his defeat, he had always pulled the shades. Her flesh, what he called her deep, rich, lovely flesh, he liked to look at, but he did not want her to see him.

She would never point out the resemblance between the flower and the man. She would never tell him just what her tiny scissors were for. Laughter would be bad enough, talk of castration would be worse.

With a snip, the anthers would be gone from the purple flower that she had decided would be the mother plant.

The next step is pollination. The anthers on the father plant had to be destroyed for this too, but somehow it was less threatening. She crushed them in her fingers so that the pollen came out, and caught it on a piece of paper. Then, she transferred the grains to the tip of the pistil on the mother plant with a tiny brush or with her fingers.

In a week or two after the transfer, she could tell if fertilization had been successful if the ovary at the base of the pistil began to swell. Then she had nothing to do but wait until the seeds had matured in six to nine months. It was almost like being pregnant.

Each time she was with child, Louise had known quickly. The tender breasts, the small ball of nausea that rose almost like excitement in her throat, a certain carefulness of being — she recognized them at least a week before the conventional sign was due. After that, she knew. She was tired, she was heavy, she knew she was sharing this body with another being. But she was also healthy; she was pleased with herself, pleased with what she was accomplishing all alone, without anyone's help. Next came a tricky time for the plantlets. Louise checked the cuttings twice a day to make sure they weren't too humid. It was a mistake to think Africa and assume humid. The East Usambara mountains, where Baron von Saint Paul-Illaire had found wild African violets, are not full of steamy forests. African violet leaves are thick and succulent like the ones you find on plants accustomed to drying out a little. Her *Saintpaulia*, her African violets, her *violettes d'Usambara* don't flower well when they're too wet, or if it gets too hot or too cold. They like things just right.

She smiled to herself. Just right. Being just. Being right. What Thomas had always been talking about when he campaigned. The silly man ...

The man who was missing in Africa.

Standing just outside the garden room, she saw how green and lovely the plants looked, their flowers shining against their velvety leaves. The first big, double-petalled dark red blossoms of the plant she'd saved from Thomas were beginning to unfurl. For just a second, she felt a sort of pleasure pass over her, as if she had touched the heart of something growing and been assured that everything would be all right. Then the feeling vanished.

Thomas was missing.

The driver was late, and Thomas found himself pacing the hotel garden. The barman wasn't on duty yet, and, remembering the connection between Théophile and Nzosaba, Thomas was reluctant to ask anyone just what might be happening, in case the arrangement to go to the river would be frowned upon by them. By 10 a.m., he was thoroughly bored and ready to consider going off for a walk by himself. He would go crazy if he had to spend the day cooped up in a garden. The dinner with Nzosaba and his friends was a prospect worth looking forward to, but between now and then he would have to get through the long, boring hours.

He could take a nap, even though it was morning. The thought was half-tempting because he had not slept very well. The young lady in the red dress had been charming, well-spoken and considerate, but he was too tired, too something to take her as he would have liked. Just as well, he did not have any condoms with him (Louise had packed for him, after all) and he had not thought to ask the barman if he had any for sale. The young lady might have been equipped with them, but as

THE VIOLETS OF USAMBARA

soon as he realized what was happening to him, he knew enough not
to ask her. That would make it worse. It would be easier to pretend
that he was prepared to pay for conversation.

So they talked, or rather, he encouraged her to talk, and he listened,
thinking all the time of the joke that made the rounds of trade missions every year or so — how can you tell when a third world country
will never climb out of poverty?

When the cab drivers are better educated than you are.

This girl had dreams, or once had dreams. Her father was an army
officer, killed in reprisals following the troubles of 1993. She'd been in
the convent school then, along with her three younger sisters — there
were eight children in all, she said.

Eight children. During that long lunch at the Club Nautique,
Nzosaba had said as many people lived per square kilometre in Burundi
or Rwanda as did per square kilometre in the most industrialized
and productive parts of Europe. That was a recipe for starvation,
Thomas thought, although he didn't say anything. How could you
feed so many people when all agriculture was subsistence, in a country
with no exports? As the girl talked, he wondered why anyone would
be surprised about what amounted to battles over cornfields. Too
many people on too little land equalled trouble. Everything else was
rationalization.

What, he wanted to ask, does this mean for the rest of the world?
Why are so few people asking this question? Are those of us from rich
countries going to sit around and wait until AIDS and neighbours
killing neighbours bring the population under control, while we eat
and drink and burn more than our share? How cruel and cynical and
immoral.

Where was the Church in all this? He and Louise had three children,
no more. She had made her peace with the Church over that, the
priest she consulted said it was more important to have the children
you could love than have all the children you could have. Besides, he
overheard Louise say to their cleaning woman that the doctor who

invented the birth control pill was Catholic, and the Pope took too long to decide that it was not right.

Obviously, that line of discourse was not current here, nor in many other parts of the world. The briefing papers said that major Muslim groups didn't believe in birth control either.

He did not say anything aloud about religion or planning families to either Nzosaba or the girl, however.

She said her mother had decided the best strategy for them was to make sure at least one of her children was trained abroad, so all of the family's excess funds went to supporting Guillaume, who was studying medicine at Howard University in the United States.

"He'll do well," the girl said. "He'll be a brilliant doctor, and he'll help the rest of us. In the meantime, the rest of us do what we can." She had smoothed her red dress over her legs as she said that, then patted her carefully straightened hair. Thomas thought briefly about telling her that his own daughter was studying medicine at Laval, but decided that would be too cruel. So would the other question he wanted to ask — did her mother know just how she was earning her contribution?

She left at about 2 a.m., and at the time, he didn't think about where she might go afterward. He didn't remember about the curfew until morning, when he started pacing around the hotel garden. Where had she slept? With another man, or wrapped up in a tablecloth on a chaise longue by the swimming pool, like the person he had seen the night before?

He would push that possibility from his mind. In fact, he might do well to push away all thought of her. Not that he counted what had happened as a betrayal of Louise, particularly considering the way it had turned out. Today, though, should be a day to think of Louise.

He tried to imagine what she would look like when she saw the fax from him. When she was pleased, her cheeks always turned rosy and her eyes danced, even now when they were both so much older.

She wouldn't see the fax until tomorrow; she wouldn't be back in Montreal until then. Maybe he could surprise her and book a call to her for the weekend. Maybe he and the others on the mission would be in circumstances where it was easier to telephone.

He looked at his watch — ten forty-five. The driver had better hurry up or they would not have time to explore properly.

In fact, it was nearly noon before they left the hotel. The driver was a small man, at least three inches shorter than Thomas, with his index and middle fingers missing from his right hand. He did not appear to be armed, but once they were outside the hotel and Thomas had paid the agreed fee, he asked the man about it.

"In the trunk," he said. "They don't know me well here, they might not like to see me with my weapon." His car was a slightly aging white BMW with the steering wheel on the right side.

"Nice car," Thomas said, as the man led him around to the back.

The man nodded. "From Dubai," he said. "BMW's the best." He opened the trunk slightly, so that Thomas had to bend over to look inside. "Uzi," he said. "Also the best. Much better than AK–47s. Israeli, not Russian."

Thomas nodded, but he had no idea. "You'll take it out later?" he asked.

"As soon as we're out of town. Don't worry. I know what I'm doing."

"Good," Thomas said, and wondered what he was getting himself into.

The day looked less unsettled than the day before. There were clouds across the lake towards Zaire, but watery sun shone on Bujumbura. They drove down the hill from the hotel, past the mosque that the background documents said Moammar Gadhafi had paid for, then out onto the flood plain and past the brewery. Thomas looked for signs of damage from the bomb blast, but from the car he couldn't see any. Passing the plant reminded Thomas that he hadn't asked about lunch. "Last night your friend said fifteen dollars of the fee was for food. We got a later start than I expected, where do you propose we stop to eat?"

"Oh, I have a very good lunch with me, first class lunch put up by caterers from the best restaurant. Hard-boiled eggs and bananas, bottled juices, beer, everything very clean and guaranteed healthy." He began to steer toward the edge of the road, cutting off men on bicycles loaded high with forage for animals. "Time to get out the Uzi anyway," he said. "I'll show you what I have."

An old wicker picnic basket, which Thomas had not noted before, sat next to the assault rifle in the trunk. "Look inside. Best of everything," the man said, lifting the lid. "Very clean."

Thomas was a little dubious about the cakes wrapped in cloth, but he merely nodded.

"It wouldn't be safe to stop just anywhere to eat," the driver said. "Have to think of safety."

"Fine, fine," Thomas said, looking out at the steady stream of bicycle and foot traffic that was passing them. The bottled juice would probably be all right, as would the bananas.

A group of boys who had been carrying bundles of long grasses and branches stopped and watched what they were doing. There was a quick ripple of movement among them when the driver took the lid off the basket, showing the food inside. They moved back quickly when the driver brandished the weapon at them. "Boys from the camps," he said. "Don't trust them."

Who should you trust? Thomas noticed that two of the boys appeared to have long keloid scars on their legs, showing bright pink against their dark skin, the tracks of machetes. "Let's get going," he said.

The driver put the Uzi in a rack he had rigged between the two seats in the front, and they started out again. The windows were all open, and they went so fast that the sound of rushing air made conversation difficult. They had passed the turnoff to the airport and were heading through what looked like fields in ordinary times before

THE VIOLETS OF USAMBARA

the driver spoke again. "We should start looking along the banks of the river," he said. "There are many plants along the river."

Thomas watched while he shifted down so they could turn onto an unpaved track that led westward. The man's right hand was marked with pink keloids at the stumps of the fingers. Did he shoot from his left shoulder using his left hand to pull the trigger, or had he trained the ring finger on his right hand? Did the fact that he had to compensate mean he was slower to react? What would that mean in a time of difficulty? Would it be smart to turn around and go back, before they'd gone too far off the track?

"After we finish," the driver said, "after you find what you're looking for, we could stop at a place I know for refreshment. Very nice place." He paused. "Very nice ladies."

The barman must have told him about the girl in the red dress. It wasn't like that at all, he almost said. He didn't, he knew that it might have been different. All the more reason to go on, to find the plants, to bring one back for Louise.

She turned and walked back through the kitchen. She picked up the telephone handset and carried it with her while she walked through the quiet house. Frédéric would be awake soon. There were many more calls to make. She wanted to make sure she could answer immediately if anyone called her.

In the living room, she saw they had forgotten to shut the curtains the night before. As well, her suitcase still sat by the front door where she'd left it when she came in less than twenty-four hours ago. A stack of newspapers lay on the coffee table — Rosa had saved them all while she was away, so she could read them. She had always considered reading papers a big part of her job, and even now she kept an eye out for interesting stories and cut out things she thought Thomas shouldn't miss. It helped her work, too. Nobody else knew as much about the charity situation as she did, knowing which companies prospered did help when it came to fundraising.

She was not ready to sit down and begin plowing through the stack, though. She crossed over to the windows to look out at the street. The pale blue sky was illuminated by the rising sun — it would be a nice day, with light that hurt the eyes. By evening, there might not be much of the new snow left. Winter was ending. All the signs were there — look, not yet six thirty and already you could read by the light outside.

The Ribeira Chà truck was parked up near the corner. Usually Manny parked it closer to the store, but with the snow piles perhaps he couldn't find a closer spot. There he was, hurrying around the corner, rubbing his hands together, dressed in a light jacket with nothing on his head. He'll be cold; he'll catch cold, he should be careful, what would Rosa do if he came down with something terrible?

Louise watched as he walked around the truck to see if any snow had been pushed up against it during the night. There was a pile by the right front wheel where the person who had parked in front had dug out his car, leaving a mound a half-metre high that hadn't been there when Manny parked. Hadn't Rosa said he was supposed to meet someone this morning at the Central Market?

Louise watched him take a shovel from the back of the truck, and with a few quick movements, dig out the wheel. He was a strong man, not so young anymore — he must be in his late thirties — but direct and honest, she'd always thought. Born in São Miguel, but here since he was five or six, an immigrant success story. Except that he wasn't a success, and the store, his dream — "Madame Brossard, you may think I'm crazy, but I don't think there's any better work than making it easier for people to feed their families well," he told her once — was becoming a nightmare.

He climbed in the truck and turned on the engine. Louise could hear the noise through the window in the morning quiet. Then he got out again and scraped off the frost that had settled on the windshield overnight and checked to be sure that snow was not covering the headlights.

He was just about ready to get back in when the man came up behind him. Louise did not see where he had been waiting, probably in the car on the corner, which she now saw was running and sending a small cloud of water vapour into the air, and ordinarily she would have turned away in order not to intrude. She didn't, perhaps because she was already so deeply caught up in the Da Silvas' lives, so she saw the discussion that went on between the two, although she did not hear the words. She saw the little man raise his fist, she saw Manny put his own hand up to stop it, she saw the scuffle, she saw, suddenly, the effect that something the man shouted had on Manny.

172 | He stopped, he stared, and then he turned back toward the man's car, which indeed was the one on the corner. After that, Louise could not see what happened, although she stood, watching for several more minutes.

Then, at three minutes after seven, the telephone rang.

Tuesday, March 18, 1997
Réserve naturelle de Ruzizi, Burundi.

Thomas

As the BMW jounced along the track toward the river, Thomas thought
of the last time he had collected a plant for Louise. That had been six
years ago, on a Sunday about this time of year, or maybe a little later.

The snow had already disappeared, even in shadowy places, and he
found himself sweating in the first warmth of spring as they walked
up from Louise's parent's house. They'd all been there for Sunday
dinner, and the next day he was going off to Mexico and then on to
Chile for free trade negotiations. He was right in the thick of things
back then. Before he left, though, Louise said she wanted time alone
with him.

She was already so heavy that he had started to worry about her.
Carrying around all that weight couldn't be good for her health, but
he knew she wouldn't listen to him if he approached the topic head-
on. Appealing to her sense of duty might work. He might say that he
depended on her, that she had to stay healthy for him. If he mentioned
her looks, he knew that she would only flare up at him and then sulk
the whole time he was gone.

She'd suggested the walk, however, that he remembered clearly, which showed that she was thinking about what was happening to her body, even though she didn't say anything. Certainly it had been a grand day for a walk. He remembered how they had stopped after the first part of the climb, at a spot where they could look out and see the trees and houses of Outremont and the imitation gothic tower of Sainte-Anne-d'Outremont, the mosque-like dome and minaret of Saint-Michel-de-Mile-End and the blue sky and grey clouds leading the eye up and over the city toward the low row of mountains in the distance.

They'd been holding hands, and he had kidded her about how he was going to have to pull her up the rest of the way if she didn't start to move a little faster. So they'd continued past the big, grey stone houses, set in big gardens, on the way to the mountain. The first crocuses were up, as well as a few snowdrops and other plants, whose names he didn't know but Louise had smiled at, longingly.

"Just you wait," he said to her. "Give me another term in office and I'll retire to a bunch of directorships and we'll buy a house up here. Anyone you want, with the biggest garden of them all."

"With a conservatory on the south side, like that one there," she said, pointing to a house on the corner. There were a few red flowers in it — poinsettias, maybe, those ones you see at Christmas time everywhere — but not much else. "It's a crime to have a room like that and not do more with it," she said. "Think what I've done with our garden room. It was not much more than a shed really, in the beginning. Can you imagine what I could do with that?"

He put his arm around her and turned her back toward the sidewalk so she'd continue walking up the hill. Her skin was smooth on her cheeks, the fresh air turning them pink the way he liked.

"So you see why I should soldier on a little longer," he said. "You understand why I've got to travel. These treaties are important, they'll make a big difference ..."

"Yes, yes, I understand," she said. "Although, you ought to read some of the liberation theologians before you go to Mexico. There may be problems ..."

"There always will be problems," he said. "That's life."

They turned right at Mont Royal Boulevard, along a flat stretch past more houses and broad lawns still brown from the winter. At the end, where the street turned down around the convent, a path took off through the woods to the top of the mountain. Part of the land belonged to the nuns who ran the convent school and part to the Protestant cemetery. Neither had developed it, so it remained wilder than nearly any other place on the island of Montreal. As they approached, Thomas saw a splash of green beneath the trees — the first leaves of something, interspersed with white flowers.

"Trillium," Louise said. "Look, how lovely!" She put out her hand for Thomas to help her over the boulders that had been piled across the path to keep out motorcycles and all-terrain vehicles. "I want to see."

She balanced teeteringly on the top of the rock before she jumped down. She landed slightly wrong, her ankle bending under her. He knew what had happened before she did, seeing the way tears welled-up in her eyes from the pain. "Sit down," he said. "You've turned something."

She hobbled over to a flat part of the rock and sat down. He knelt in front of her and rubbed her ankle gently. Not broken, he was sure, and probably with a little help she'd get home all right. "You sit here and put your foot up," he said, dragging over part of a stump that stuck out between the rocks. "I'll go find you a walking stick to help you get home."

She bit her lip to keep from crying, but nodded her head. "Why is it," she said, "that every time I try to do something carefree and impulsive, I hurt myself or someone else? Why can't I be a little more ethereal?"

He laughed. Ethereal was not the word for her and never had been. "Don't laugh at me," he heard her say as he started up the trail. "Why don't you ever take me seriously? Don't leave me," she said. "Don't you ever leave me."

He found a good, stout stick not ten metres further up the path, but on the way back down, he also saw a flat stone that looked almost like a shovel blade. The bed of trilliums was only a few steps away on the hillside. He didn't even get his boots wet as he scrambled over and used the stone to dig up four plants. He wrapped the roots in a scarf he had stuffed in his pocket.

Louise planted the trilliums in the shady part at the end of the garden. He thought they were still there, still blooming.

But the driver continued to talk about the women at the place he wanted to stop. "Fine girls, very *sympathique*," he said.

"No," Thomas said. "I'm on a mission for my wife."

He'd expected an African jungle to be impenetrable and dark, but this was both lighter and more familiar than anything he'd seen in the movies. There were a few big palms, but most of the trees were tall, thin leafy ones. Ferns grew from rocks that stuck out of the soil. He thought of the Laurentians in summer. Hot and full of life, but not depressing, not oppressive.

There were few flowers, and of course, he really did not know where to look for violets. He had the driver stop here and stop there so he could get out to investigate, but after a couple of hours, it was clear that the driver was finding the whole exercise fruitless.

"Let us go back to the place I was telling you about. There are many flowers there, nice garden, sweet smelling things."

"No," Thomas said flatly. He straightened up and looked around him. He had no idea where to look next. He began to think that perhaps he wouldn't be able to recognize an African violet if he saw one. "What have you got to drink?" he asked. "Let's have some of that juice, or the beer in your lunch."

The driver gladly opened the trunk and dragged the lunch basket out. They stood, leaning against the car and drinking. The beer was hot, but it still felt good going down. Thomas drank two bottles quickly and then told the driver to drive a little closer to the river. "If we don't find anything there, we'll go back," he said.

By the time Thomas had finished looking along the road near the river and then along the river bank, the sun was low over the hills in Zaire. The driver leaned against the BMW with his cap pushed down low on his face to shield his eyes from the slanting rays that filtered through the leaves. He looked half asleep, despite the fact that he was standing upright with the Uzi hanging from his shoulder. Thomas had been bent over, searching along the side of a little rivulet. When he straightened up, he saw the men before the driver did.

At first glance, he thought there were no more than five or six of them, but as the space around the car began to fill with men slipping out of the forest shadows, Thomas had to guess more — ten, twenty, thirty, even.

They were dressed in shorts and T-shirts. Most carried machetes, whose blades they touched lightly when they saw who they had before them. They looked at Thomas as if he were part of the landscape.

Then they looked at the driver, who became aware of their eyes all at once. His body snapped to attention, as if struck by a whip. He looked around himself carefully. He tested a smile. He pointed to Thomas.

The white man was no shelter. The men in front of the group said something in a language that Thomas did not understand. The driver reached in his pocket and pulled out papers. He shuffled through them, then handed two or three to the men who seemed to be in charge.

The men with the machetes moved the blades slightly, the way the tip of a cat's tail will twitch when it is stalking. The two with AK–47s did not move. That was when Thomas realized that whatever this was, it was not considered important enough to waste ammunition. They were losers, on the fringes of a bloody conflict. War over a cornfield, over a rice paddy. The future for us all?

No, he thought, whatever this is, I am important enough to be shot. He lunged toward the man nearest him.

The driver crossed himself and moved. Thomas felt nothing but the impact in his ears from the sound of a discharging AK–47. He saw the driver stepping forward to return fire with his Uzi. He saw the blood surging upward from the chest of the man. He saw blood blooming in front of his own eyes. He saw the purple and red blossoms of blood.

178 | It was nearly nightfall when Thomas opened his eyes. He'd been dreaming, he thought. A memory of soft flesh and snowy afternoons, open mouths and Louise lay at the edge of his consciousness.

He looked up through the leaves at the sky. Gathering clouds or the setting sun? Would it rain?

He heard no voices. He felt no pain. Only a great tiredness settling over him. Should he be alarmed? Was he coming down with one of those tropical diseases?

This had nothing to do with being ill. And yes, of course, he should be alarmed. He was a fool not to be alarmed. He was, perhaps, a fool, *tout court*. He forced his eyes to remain open and so, high above him, he saw the first wave of the creatures he had thought were waterfowl, heading south.

He had come looking for African violets, the *violettes d'Usumbura*, for Louise, and that shadow over there, just at the edge of his field of vision, was the driver who had brought him to this place, this forest by a river, in a country where people hated each other so. The driver must be lying where he fell, another victim in a war whose rules Thomas would never know.

He had not found the violets, and he would never bring a wild plant to Louise, never hear her little chirps of pleasure, never feel her press herself close to him. In spite of all he'd done, he loved her, he wanted to please her.

Remember how he'd dug those trilliums for her and carried them home in his scarf, while he supported her hobbling form down the hillside. At the bottom, on Côte-Sainte-Catherine, he'd hailed a cab, and they'd arrived home as the early spring sun was setting. The cool air had been good for her ankle, the doctor said the next morning when Thomas took her in to have it looked at. Nothing serious, a simple sprain. She was told to take some ibuprofen and stay off it for a few days. And so, Thomas had arranged to remain in Montreal a little longer than he'd planned, so he could fetch and carry for her. Poor thing, poor darling. She'd used the time to read his background papers for the negotiations and had made several good suggestions, suggestions which unfortunately nobody took seriously. Too bad — would they have won the next election if it weren't for NAFTA?

And the trillium. She had been so pleased ...

Now that the light was fading around him, he could not tell himself that she'd been pleased. She had not. She had yelled at him. "They are protected flowers," she screamed. "You can't go digging them up just any place you find them. You can't always do the first thing that occurs to you, you've got to think sometimes. What do you do when I'm not around?"

But she'd planted them, hadn't she? They would bloom in a few weeks, although he knew that he wouldn't be there to see them.

The silent birds continued to pass above him. He stared, trying to make sense of them, and of everything else, until they were transformed into swirling snowflakes, into whirling atoms, into a shower of shooting stars.

The sun was rising. The amplified call to prayer poured out of the mosque to the left as Louise stood at the second floor window of the guest house. She had finished her own morning prayers and, once again, was reading the last fax from Thomas. Rosa had found it in the pile of scratch paper when she came to clean before the memorial service. Louise still shivered at the thought that it might have been thrown out with the rest of the trash, cleaned away with the detritus of several days of worry and sorrow.

It hadn't, thank goodness. It was her last link with Thomas and she treasured it, even though what she held was not the original. She'd carried that one around until the paper had begun to fray along the fold lines. Sylvain had several photocopies made and had them encased in flexible plastic so she could fold the fax again and again. In the four years since, she'd worn through three, but Sylvain said he would always keep her supplied.

He had gone back to Montreal, so he was going to miss seeing the wild African violets, not that he cared that much. "They're your thing, Maman," he told her when they were planning this trip. "Frédéric and I will see that you get to Africa. I'll stay around for a few days after the ceremonies in Bujumbura, but then I've got to get back in time to start school."

She couldn't argue with that. If he'd finally decided it was worth his time to study, she couldn't stand in his way. She was pleased that Frédéric accompanied them to Bujumbura for the presentation of the first Thomas Brossard Scholarship; she understood why neither Richard nor Marielle could get away. She was amazed that she was now on her own in Africa.

The view out the window was not inspiring. The sea was behind her and the East Usambara mountains, forty kilometres away, were hidden by trees and whitewashed buildings dating from more than a half century ago, when Tanga was the centre of sisal production. As she watched, the last of the bats swooped toward the building across the street, where they appeared to make their home during the day in its vacant upper stories. The young naturalist from the Université de Montréal had told her about them. He'd met her at the airport in Dar es Salaam, driven her the five hours to Tanga, and then seen that she'd safely checked into the hotel. He stood at this same window the night before and pointed out flights of bats leaving for a night of catching insects on the wing. Bats were his specialty.

"Did you see the big fruit bats in Bujumbura?" he asked. "There's a mountain north of the city where they spend their days and at sunset you can see thousands and thousands of them flying silently overheard."

She hadn't seen them, and was glad she hadn't. "Bats," she said. "Thousands and thousands of bats? No, thank you."

He'd laughed. "Oh, like so much in this world, they're better than the press they get. Malaria would be a lot worse if it weren't for those guys out there eating mosquitoes. And the fruit bats around Bujumbura don't do anyone harm."

Be that as it may, she was not disappointed that no one had pointed them out to her during the two weeks she and Sylvain had been in Burundi.

Another muezzin began his chant, this one a little farther to the north. Louise put Thomas's message back in the little pouch where she carried her precious things, and started to pack what she had taken out of her suitcase the night before. The naturalist had said he'd come to fetch her at about six thirty — the trip to the Amani Nature Reserve, where the wild African violets grew, took about two hours on the mountain roads, he said, and they had been invited for a working breakfast with the staff.

Frédéric had arranged this part of the trip. One of his architect friends had designed the glass conservatory that sheltered plants from East Africa at the botanical garden in Ottawa, and when Frédéric said his cousin's dream had been to visit the African violet's natural habitat, he'd made all the necessary introductions. Louise was thankful for his help because, even with her newly discovered courage, she didn't know if she could have survived the trip from Bujumbura to Tanzania alone — two flights, three airports, plus the overland journey. Luckily, Frédéric's friend knew just who would help in each place.

She had come a long way, in every possible sense of the word. Geographically, the distance was thousands of kilometres. Spiritually, it had been an even longer journey since the day, six weeks after Thomas's death, when Rosa found her in the kitchen. From the outside, it must have seemed that she had begun to recover by then. Nearly all of the paperwork dealing with Thomas's insurance and will was complete, his ashes sat on the mantel, waiting for Louise and the children to decide where they should go. Louise was going to early Mass and working on her projects for the rest of the day. Frédéric dropped in frequently to see how she was doing and share a drink or two. The children called at least once a week. In short, it appeared that things were on their way back to normal.

But when Rosa came in that day, Louise was sitting in the over-stuffed reclining rocker she'd had Sylvain drag into the kitchen right after the funeral. Her head was leaning against its high back, her eyes were closed, her mouth open. Her legs were spread apart, as if she had never heard nuns lecture about the way one should sit. On the table next to her were piled five plates and an assortment of cutlery, all dirty. Empty bottles and fast food cartons littered the counter. It looked as if she hadn't picked up anything since Rosa had come to clean two days before. It looked, in fact, as if Louise had not moved for some time, and for an awful second, Rosa said later, she wondered if Louise were still alive. Then Louise stirred and opened her eyes. She blinked and looked in Rosa's direction, but gave no sign of recognition. Instead, she turned her head slowly until her gaze landed on a glass on the table next to her. It was coated with fingerprints, but a little clear liquid remained in the bottom. She reached out for it and brought it carefully to her lips. She shut her eyes again as she drank what was left, as if wanting to savour it. But as she swallowed, her eyes snapped open. "Melted ice cubes," she said. "Rosa, can you get me something more to drink?"

"No," Rosa said, the first time she had ever refused Louise anything.

"Look at you," she said. "This has gone too far. Look at what you are becoming." She took Louise's face between her hands and turned it so Louise could not avoid her reflection in the window of the garden room.

She had trouble focusing, and the light wasn't right for the reflection to be sharp, but through the fog filling her head, she knew exactly what she would see — the same fat woman with frizzy hair who was always there. But a woman who had changed in some important ways. A woman who knew that it was highly unlikely she would ever again be loved by a man, or that someone's eyes would light up when he saw her, or that someone's hand would slide up the inside of her thigh, higher and higher, until the world contained only the two of them, and shooting stars. She would see in her reflection, she knew, a woman who was finding it very difficult to continue to believe. A woman on whom the weight of guilt had begun to press, who suspected that she had much to blame herself for. Neither prayer nor the beauty of her *violettes d'Usambara* were able to comfort her anymore.

Rosa braced her feet and took Louise's hands. "Get up," she said. "You have to get up." When Louise was on her feet, Rosa half pushed her, half led her upstairs and into the bathroom. She turned on the shower. "Get in," she said. "I'll bring you clean clothes, these look like you've been wearing them for days."

She had, Louise remembered afterwards. When she came back down, Rosa had washed the dirty dishes, made tea and brought out her rosary. "We will pray together," she said, "we will ask God for help."

Louise did not object. When Rosa gestured toward her big chair, she sat down in it and put her head back on the cushion. The clock ticked and the light from outside moved slowly across the kitchen as the afternoon advanced. Once, Rosa paused in her prayers and looked over at her, but when Louise said nothing, she continued. Then finally, as if it had taken a very long time for her to decide to act, Louise leaned forward, pushing her body away from the back of the chair, so she could reach across the table. She hesitated again, and then placed her hand lightly on Rosa's forearm.

Rosa stopped, letting the beads hang from her fingers.

"You know," Louise whispered, "he wouldn't have gone if I hadn't insisted. It was my idea." The words came out with great difficulty, she could hardly pronounce them. "I am to blame," she said. It was a thought that she had never formulated concretely before, arranged in sentences she would never say again.

Rosa stopped and put down her rosary. She took Louise's hand in hers and held it without saying anything for several minutes.

"It is not your fault," Rosa said at last. She looked straight into Louise's eyes. "He wouldn't have gone if he hadn't wanted to. He would have found an excuse."

Louise looked away. It was true he had not thought up reasons for why he should not go, and before he had always been good at evading what he didn't want to do. Think how he escaped to Ottawa all those times when she was angry, how he left her in the Museé des beaux-arts after he had tricked her into being nice to the Bührles.

"Look at me," Rosa said, and touched Louise's face with her free hand, guiding it so it turned and their eyes met again. "It was the same with Manny. I begged him not to take that money, but he said he had to. He wanted me to think it was the answer to my prayers." She swallowed, suddenly her voice had become hoarse. "The answer to my prayers!" she repeated. "As if God would be mixed-up in that kind of business!" She dropped Louise's hand. "But you did what you had to do. I did too," she said when she could speak again. "No one can ask more than that, not even God."

"Yes," Louise said after a moment, after she had considered what God might ask, "but what do I do now?"

Rosa reached into her pocket for a tissue. She blew her nose and looked over at Louise again. "What you can do. Not drink so much, to begin with."

Agreed, although it was a struggle to stop, as hard as trying not to let panic overwhelm her. The drink had kept the panic at bay, she didn't feel the menace waiting outside as sharply, she didn't feel as much, *tout court.*

Frédéric understood, as might someone who had spent many dark nights paralyzed before the conflicts in his own nature. Their long afternoons and evenings together ended. He came for dinner occasionally, he escorted her to Mass most Sundays and he began to talk of doing something in memory of Thomas.

When Louise approached him for advice, Brother Jean-Marie agreed, hinting that a fund to further the work of the Fellowship of Saint Laurent in Thomas's name might be appropriate, but Frédéric said "no" emphatically — Thomas might have good memories of the Île d'Orléans and that Sunday he met Louise, but Brother Jean-Marie's retreat was her business, not his. The children suggested a scholarship fund at UMass or McGill, where Thomas had studied, or support for mother-child clinics, or an anti-AIDS initiative, but none of those ideas seemed right to Louise either.

It took a letter of condolence from Sylvain's friend Benjamin before Louise began to see the way. "*Madame Brossard,*" Benjamin wrote the autumn following Thomas's death, "*Forgive my tardiness, but I've been studying in Toronto and heard the news about M. Brossard last week when I was back in Montreal. I only met him a few times, but I will never forget the weekend I spent with you in the terrible days after my own father's death. I don't think I thanked you then — kids don't do things like that — but I want to say now that your kindness meant a lot to me. Please give Sylvain my best wishes, and tell him that perhaps I understand what he's going through. He should give me a call the next time he's in Toronto.*"

The boy whose father was from Rwanda and who had come to study in Montreal. It seemed so obvious now that Louise almost laughed. Why hadn't she thought of it before? The thing to do would be to provide a way for bright young people from Burundi to study here.

The others agreed. Frédéric's partner said he would take care of setting up bank accounts, and another friend offered to do the legal work. Frédéric would make a substantial contribution, of course, but where would the rest of the money come from?

At first, Louise thought she could do it the way she did everything else, with phone calls and letters. Why not? She'd run much of Thomas's campaigns that way, she'd raised funds for other causes. Then, however, the enormity of the task hit her. To provide a fellowship that would pay $30,000 Canadian a year for graduate study — "it has to be that much," insisted Richard, who knew about graduate study because he'd recently finished his own. "Any less wouldn't cover fees and living expenses." This meant a fund of one million dollars or more. A few friends, a few contacts would contribute on the strength of no more than a request, but Louise soon discovered that to get the kind of money the fund needed, she was going to have to make appointments to see possible donors, to visit their offices, to beg.

But she couldn't do that. She panicked. She was a recluse; she had lived all her life through others, through Thomas, after all. Finally, after much prayer, she decided that if Thomas could die for a good cause, she could live for one.

She had to call Brian Mulroney to say she wanted to take him up on his offer of help. She went to a lunch with friends of Mila's and gave them her prospectus. She talked to the politicos at the federal and municipal parties, she even approached the Bührle family foundation — but only at the end, only when she had exhausted all her contacts and she needed another $50,000 to make an endowment large enough.

How Thomas would laugh at the list of donors. It was all conscience money, he'd say, and he'd be right. Conscience money has its uses, however, as Frédéric always said.

He'd been a good travelling companion, and so had Sylvain. The three of them saw a lot — the cathedral in Bujumbura, of course, and, after he had left, visits to a couple of model cattle farms set up by a charity based in Montreal, and a trip to a centre for malnourished babies near Gitega, run by Canadian nuns. One of them remembered talking to Thomas when the observation team visited the camp where she was working. "Such a big-hearted man," she said. "He was so concerned about the children."

Louise was pleased to hear that because, even in Bujumbura, she learned very little news about the circumstances of his death. Monsieur Nzosaba, the businessman who arranged a reception for them at the Club Nautique, told her Thomas was thinking of her at the last, hoping to bring her back a flower. What flower she couldn't imagine, because she knew so little about the flora of Central Africa.

The phone rang.

"Can you be ready in ten minutes, Madame Brossard?" the naturalist said when she answered.

"Of course, of course," she said. It was her turn now. She was free to do what she'd dreamed of doing ever since she became interested in African violets. She was going to see, finally, her *violettes d'Usambara* in the wild.

When he hung up, Louise sat by the window for a moment longer, with the sound of the muezzin still in her ears. By then, the bats had all gone to roost, small creatures that were not what they appeared to be. The sun began to disperse the mist that had settled along the coast during the night. Louise thought she could see better, she thought she understood what was going on.

Acknowledgements

With many thanks to le Conseil des arts et lettres du Québec for its financial support during the year in which this book was researched and partly written; to Léo Kalinda, the late Bonaventure Murigande, Jean-Claude Simard, William Hartzog and William Schabas, who gave me their impressions and much good advice before I went to Africa; to my neighbours Jean-Louis Bolduc and Nicola Bridge, who made sure I had a hotel reservation and contact telephone numbers before I left; to Libère Nahimana, his daughter Francine and her husband Alain Mandi, whose hospitality in Bujumbura was as generous as it was unexpected; to Louis-Robert Daigle and Claudie Senay of the Canadian Department of Foreign Affairs and International Trade, who let me tag along; and, as always, to Lukas, Elin and Lee.

I owe a great debt to the journalists of Net Press, who provided a daily news summary of what was happening in Burundi for several years, which told me much about the political climate there in March and April, 1997. It should be noted that I have switched the order of the attacks near Bujumbura for the purposes of my story: this should not reflect on the accuracy of Net Press's chronology. Other sources: *The Passionate Eye: Impressionist and Other Master Paintings from the*

E.G. Bührle Collection, the catalogue for the exhibition in commemoration of the 100th birthday of the collector Emil G. Bührle (Zurich, Artemis, 1990); Courtemanche, Gil, *Un dimanche à la piscine à Kigali* (Montréal, Boréal, 2000); Gourivetch, Philip, *We Wish to Inform You That Tomorrow We Will Be Killed with Our Families* (New York, Farrar, Straus and Giroux, 1998); Lemarchand, René, *Burundi: Ethnic Conflict and Genocide* (Cambridge, Woodrow Wilson Center Press and Cambridge University Press, 1994); and Off, Carol, *The Lion, the Fox and the Eagle: A Story of Generals and Justice in Yugoslavia and Rwanda* (Toronto, Random House Canada, 2000).

Thanks also are due to Anne Richard who invited me, Elin, and Lukas to the Île d'Orléans when my children and her children, Victoire and Gabriel, were little; to three other *filles de bonne famille* — Louise DesForges, Danielle Naltchayan, and Andrée Tousignant — who answered my questions about what a girl like Louise might read and about her family's domestic arrangements; to the other Durochères (Thérèse Decelles-Fortin, Jacqueline DePlaen, Aloyse du Pasquier, Monique Hamelin, Debby Harris, Élisabeth Humbolt, Dominique LeClercq, Rollande Pelletier and Antoinette Savoie) for their friendship and support over many years; to my writing friends Ann Charney, David Helwig, David Homel, Julie Keith and Fred Reed who read various early drafts of the story, and to Marc Côté who asked good questions about it.